The Blue Bottle

By Emilie-Noelle Provost

North Country Press

The Blue Bottle

ISBN 978-1-943424-42-9

Library of Congress Control Number: 2018955741

Cover art by Lucy Turner, Scotland, UK

North Country Press
Unity, Maine

For Madelaine

Chapter 1

Charlotte stared out the bus window as it sped past sumac trees and weeds as tall as a man's waist, all swaying in the afternoon breeze. She'd been to visit her grandparents in Rocky Harbor, a small village on Cape Ann, many times before, but this was the first time she was going alone.

Charlotte lived in a worn out factory town in central Massachusetts, in a sagging duplex with her father and older brother, Charles. Mr. Clark, the principal at Charlotte's school, had sent home a note the week before, during the last week of school, recommending that she attend a summer program for kids who have trouble with math. She'd barely made it out of the seventh grade because of her D- average in pre-algebra.

Charlotte's father said Mr. Clark should mind his own business. Instead of filling out the registration form, he bought Charlotte a bus ticket.

Charlotte felt a tap on her shoulder. A woman about her grandmother's age had taken the seat beside her. Her auburn hair, streaked with gray, was pulled into a bun held in place with a wooden comb.

"I'll bet you're Ben and Ava's granddaughter," the woman said.

Charlotte nodded.

"I'm Marie Bouchard. I used to teach third grade at Rocky Harbor Elementary. Your father was one of my students."

Surprised, Charlotte said, "Nice to meet you."

Mrs. Bouchard leaned down and pulled two knitting needles and a skein of sky-blue yarn from a canvas bag at her feet. "I make hats for the newborns at Cape Ann Hospital. Keeps me busy now that I'm retired."

Charlotte watched as the shiny needles flashed. After a few minutes, a circle—what would become the top of a baby's hat—began to form.

"How did you learn to do that?" Charlotte's mother could barely sew a button.

"I've been knitting since I was younger than you are," said Mrs. Bouchard "My mother taught me. Would you like to try?"

Mrs. Bouchard reached into her bag and pulled out another set of needles. Placing them in Charlotte's hands, she said, "Hold them like this. Don't bend your thumb."

They were heavy and awkward. Charlotte struggled to get her yarn to do anything even close to what Mrs. Bouchard's was doing. "I don't think I can do it," she said finally.

"I hope you don't give up on everything so quickly. I'll tell you what. Next Tuesday my grandson is coming to stay with me. He's about your age. Why don't you come over and I'll give you both a knitting lesson."

Charlotte pictured the three of them sitting out on the porch knitting baby hats. Maybe she should have tried harder to convince her father to let her stay home.

When Mrs. Bouchard lifted her bag to place Charlotte's yarn and needles back inside, something hard skittered onto the floor. Charlotte bent down to pick it up and found a small glass bottle the color of a sapphire lying beneath the seat in front of her.

"What's this?" she said.

"Oh, that's just something I use when I do story time at the library. It's not the real thing, of course. But the little ones like to pass it around. I thought I'd lost it. I must have put it in my knitting bag by mistake. Has your grandmother told you the story of the blue bottle?"

"I don't think so," said Charlotte.

Mrs. Bouchard arched her eyebrows. "Well, I think it's time you heard it, especially since you'll be in Rocky Harbor for a while."

She set her knitting in her lap and began to tell Charlotte the story:

"Sometime in the late 1700s, a woman named Ruth Smith lived in a cottage at the edge of Gertrude's Cove. Back in those days Rocky Harbor was just a small fishing village and the town didn't have a doctor.

"Because Ruth wasn't married and had no children, she took care of people in town as a way to support herself. She knew everything there was to know about herbal medicines and the sorts of cures that come from the sea. She delivered all Rocky Harbor's babies, and some in nearby towns, too. Her ability to cure the sick was regarded by some as miraculous – and by others as a bit sinister. Some of the ladies in the village whispered that Ruth was a witch.

"Ruth's people, some used to say, were from an ancient line. Not from Europe like most of the townspeople's ancestors, but from the sea itself. Ruth's forebears were believed to be those creatures, half human and half fish, that lived beneath the cove.

"One day, when Ruth was still quite young, she was sent to care for an elderly woman who'd had a terrible fall. Her house was deep in the woods, down a narrow path and away from the main part of the village.

"This woman was the oldest person Ruth had ever seen. Her skin was nearly translucent, her legs as thin as a bird's. Her pale blue eyes had a dullness to them as she sat in a high-backed wooden chair, wrapped in a woolen shawl in spite of the summer heat.

"An old fisherman told Ruth that this woman had magical powers. He said when he was young he had seen her change into a mermaid. She could talk to the creatures of the sea and the birds in the air and make them do her bidding.

"But on that day all Ruth saw was a withered woman with a puff of white hair who needed her help. An enormous bruise had formed on her left temple and her leg was badly cut.

"At first the woman said nothing as Ruth cleaned and wrapped the wound on her leg, but when Ruth had finished and was heating water over the fire to make tea, the woman, whose name no one is sure of today, began to talk.

"The story she told Ruth was even older than the woman herself:

" 'Once there was an English sea captain named Jonathan Goode who specialized in transporting merchants' wares between Rotterdam and Boston. The year was 1624 and Goode had taken on cargo from Rome for a good price, much more than such a load would normally bring. At first, the captain was glad of his good fortune – and it was true that he was known among sailing men for his good luck. But soon before his ship, the *Gertrude Chance*, was to set sail, Captain Goode began to hear ominous talk among his crew.

" 'The ship's cargo, the men said, was cursed. It had been stolen from an ancient temple to Oceanus, the god of the sea. Within the wooden crates lying below deck were golden urns and pots, glittering trinkets of all kinds, and great marble carvings of dolphins and octopus that even a very rich man would consider himself lucky to have. But the most captivating treasure of all, packed in a crate all its own, was a small bottle made of blue glass. About the size of a man's pocket watch, the bottle was said to hold within it all the power of the seas.

" 'The blue bottle, it was said, had been the cause of a battle between Oceanus and his brother, Mortimer.

" 'Once Oceanus and Mortimer had ruled the seas together, sharing the bottle's power, but Mortimer grew tired of always conferring with his brother. He wanted to rule the oceans on his own. So he stole the bottle and hid it from Oceanus at the very end of the earth, in a cave at the bottom of the sea.

" 'When Oceanus discovered what his brother had done, he sent every creature in the sea to search for him, and when he was found, Oceanus demanded Mortimer return the bottle at once. Mortimer refused, and the two brothers became locked in combat.

" 'For eleven days and eleven nights their fighting churned up the sea, creating tempests and tidal waves. On the twelfth day,

4

Oceanus defeated his brother, banishing Mortimer to live forever in darkness at the bottom of the sea.

" 'Oceanus instructed his priests to build a temple on the shore of the Mediterranean, high on a hill. There he would keep the blue bottle, protecting it on dry land where Mortimer would never be able to reach it. He put a curse on anyone, god or man, who dared to take it from that place.

" 'After hearing all this, Captain Goode became uneasy. A few of his best sailors resigned rather than cross the ocean with the blue bottle on board. But in the end Goode had a contract to fulfill and *Gertrude Chance* set sail.

" 'Goode's voyage across the Atlantic proved uneventful, putting him in a good mood on the morning of May 15 when he rounded the coast of Cape Ann, his ship less than a day's sail from Boston Harbor.

" 'But as *Gertrude Chance* came within sight of land, the weather began to turn. The sky turned from soft blue to the color of a pewter tray. The air grew cold and the wind from the southwest began to gust with all the might of the Devil.

" 'Goode ordered his men to haul down the top sail, spotting a small cove off the ship's port side. The captain pulled at the wheel with all his strength as the angry sea washed over the deck. The crew clung to the rigging, terrified.

" 'In what seemed to be a miracle, *Gertrude Chance* cleared the towering rocks and came to rest in calm water, her sailors falling to the deck in relief.

" 'But just as the men had begun to right themselves an enormous vortex formed before the bow. Twice the diameter of the ship, the whirlpool spun faster and faster, creating a roar so thunderous that the men had to shout to be heard.

" 'Seeing what was about to happen, a young seaman named Boyd Morgan scurried down the ladder into the hold. Grabbing an axe, he smashed the oak crate containing the blue bottle. He slipped the treasure into his pocket and climbed back to the top deck. Amidst the terrible screams from the other men, Morgan launched himself off the stern.

" 'The next thing Morgan knew, he was sprawled on the rocks lining the shore. *Gertrude Chance* was gone. The cove was as smooth as glass.

" 'A young girl sat beside him, her blonde hair wrapped around her bare waist. Her face was the color of milk, her cheeks as lovely as a baby's. The blue bottle rested in the palm of her hand.

" 'Morgan tried to sit up but the girl, who was much stronger than she looked, placed her hand against his chest and pushed him down. It was then Morgan noticed that instead of legs the girl had a fish's tail. He screamed, but no men were left alive to hear him.

" 'The girl pressed the bottle into Morgan's palm and told him he must hide it on dry land, where she was unable to go.

" 'Morgan hid the bottle as the mermaid instructed, drawing a map to mark the spot. When he was finished, he sat down on a rock overlooking the water.

" 'An old man wearing the tattered oil clothes of a fisherman appeared on shore. Having thought he was alone, Morgan was glad to see him.

" 'Your people have taken the blue bottle from my temple,' the fisherman said. 'But because you have proved honorable and have hidden the bottle where it will be safe from my brother, I will give you a reward. Tell me what you wish for and it shall be yours.'

" 'Morgan knew then that this was not a fisherman but Oceanus himself. He got down on his knees.

" 'Because he was very much alone, Morgan said, "My wish is for a village, full of people and good boats where I might make a living from the sea and have a wife and children to carry on my name.'

" 'Not accustomed to such modest requests, the old fisherman nodded. " 'Very well. In three days' time a ship will land in this cove carrying passengers from England. Together, you will build a village. You will have strong boats and catch many fish. The creatures that live here, the sea people who are my children, will watch over and care for you.

" 'But the blue bottle's fate will forever be tied to your village. As long as the bottle is well cared for and kept out of Mortimer's hands you will prosper. But if Mortimer should ever come to possess the bottle your village will be taken by the sea.' "

" 'This sounded fair to Morgan, so he agreed and thanked the fisherman. Within a year, the village of Rocky Harbor was built, complete with a church and schoolhouse.

" 'Morgan named the cove Gertrude after his ill-fated ship. He told no one where he had hidden the bottle, and kept the map he made of its location safely hidden. And it was in this way that Rocky Harbor became a thriving and civilized settlement.'

"When the old woman had finished telling the story to Ruth she opened a wooden box, its lid and sides painted with strange symbols. She removed a yellowed square of parchment and handed the paper to Ruth.

" 'Your people were once the same as mine,' " she said, " 'so I know you can be trusted.' "

"Ruth looked at the worn document and knew immediately it was Boyd Morgan's map. She hurried home and wrote down the story the old woman had told her, exactly as it had been said. She hid the map carefully, telling no one what had happened that day.

"Early the following morning, Ruth was woken by a boy from the village banging on her door. Thinking someone was ill, Ruth hurried to answer. But the boy handed her a note from Reverend Brown. The old woman had died during the night."

Chapter 2

Charlotte's bus pulled up to the Market Basket plaza in Rocky Harbor and with a rush of air from the brakes came to a stop. Her grandparents were waiting for her on the sidewalk. Gram wore knee-length khaki shorts and a sleeveless blouse with a pink flower design. Her reading glasses dangled from a chain around her neck.

Grandpa stood with a rolled up newspaper tucked under his arm. His dress pants (the only kind he ever wore) were the color of a pine forest. Part of his Navy tattoo, a ship's anchor faded from decades of working on a lobster boat, peeked out from beneath his left sleeve.

Charlotte's grandmother gave her a big squeeze. She smelled just the way Charlotte remembered: a combination of baby powder, coffee and roses. "You've gotten so big," she said after Charlotte pulled away. "And so pretty. Isn't she pretty, Ben?"

"Of course she's pretty," said her grandfather, shifting his newspaper. "Charlotte, show me which bags are yours and I'll put them in the car."

Charlotte's grandparents drove a 1989 Buick Regal the color of a fire engine. Charlotte had been riding in it since she was born, and it was still the biggest car she had ever seen. Its bench seats were covered in soft gray fabric that felt like the skin of a peach. And when you sat down, they swallowed you up like an old living room sofa.

Her grandfather put Charlotte's bags in the trunk. Then he climbed into the driver's seat and turned up the air conditioning. "Hot one today," he said.

Rocky Harbor hadn't changed much since Charlotte had been there at Thanksgiving. Except now the downtown sidewalks were crammed with people.

Every summer thousands of tourists came to Rocky Harbor to swim at Wampannuck Beach and visit the boutiques and restaurants downtown. On White Pier, where the fishermen moored their boats, people chartered fishing trips and rented the colorful kayaks that could be seen darting around the harbor all summer long.

Traffic moved slowly. As the old Buick sat idling at the light near the pier, Charlotte's grandmother said, "There's a new shop over there on the right: Ocean Brothers' Antiques. It opened about a month ago. The owner is from England."

As they continued on, suddenly something swift and dark ran out in front of the car. Grandpa slammed on the brakes. Lying in the street, Charlotte saw a black, uneven lump, most certainly an animal. She was sure they'd hit a dog. She jumped out of the car with her grandfather right behind her.

Whatever they'd hit, Charlotte could see right away it wasn't a dog. It wasn't like any animal she had ever seen. Its skin was shiny and wet like a seal's. Its eyes, flat discs the color of mustard, were sunken into the sides of its head. A dark liquid pooled beneath the unfortunate creature, which, clearly, was dead. The animal gave off an unbearable stench that made Charlotte pull the collar of her T-shirt over her nose.

After a few minutes a police car arrived. The traffic on Water Street was backed up all the way to Gertrude's Cove.

"What's the trouble?" A young policeman with a dark crew cut stepped out of the cruiser.

"Hit some kind of animal," said Grandpa. "Came out of nowhere. I don't even know what it is."

The officer crouched down to get a closer look. He stood up quickly, gagging from the fishy smell. "Got me. Doesn't look like someone's pet, though. Don't worry about it, sir. I'll call animal control and have it removed."

Charlotte's grandparents' house looked exactly the way it always had. A mint-colored Victorian, the house had been built right at the edge of Gertrude's Cove, its backyard sloping down to the shoreline. In front of the house were Gram's rosebushes, all of them in full bloom. When Charlotte opened the car door, the sweet scent of the flowers rushed in on a wave of warm air. Inside, the house was cool. The shades were drawn. A huge window-unit air conditioner labored away in the parlor.

"Why don't you put your things up in your room, Charlotte," said Gram, who had begun to empty the dishwasher the moment they came through the door. "Then come down for some lemonade. I just made it this morning."

The room where Charlotte slept was on the third floor of the house, in what used to be the attic before it was remodeled in the early 1900s. The house had been in her grandfather's family for almost 200 years and the story went that her great-grandmother had had the room finished so that she could rent it to bachelor fishermen.

At one end of the oblong space was a double bed covered in a bright patchwork quilt. An oak rocking chair was positioned in front of the window on the opposite side of the room. A modest writing desk was tucked beside the bed. On the bedside table was a telephone. Charlotte held the receiver to her ear to check for a dial tone. Gram must have had the phone installed since the last time she'd visited.

Sitting in the rocking chair, Charlotte could see out the window past Gertrude's Cove, all the way out to the open ocean. The water was dotted with boats: yachts and sailboats and the square-hulled wooden lobster boats Rocky Harbor was known for. If she looked carefully, Charlotte could just make out the thin, dark line to the left of the cove that was White Pier.

Back downstairs, Gram had set a glass of cold lemonade on the kitchen counter along with three sugar cookies on a small plate. Next to them was a paper napkin folded in half to form a triangle. Grandpa was on the telephone.

"Ethan, I don't give a damn what grade Charles is going into, a boy that age isn't old enough to be left alone for an entire weekend. You know the kind of trouble a kid that age can get into. I shouldn't even have to tell you … stop being so selfish. For God's sake, think about what's best for your kids—for once."

He was talking to her father.

"I just called to tell you that Charlotte got here safe, not to get into an argument—I've got half a mind to have you send her brother up here, too. It would do the boy some good to get out on the boat. Do some real work. Then you and that barfly girlfriend of yours can do whatever the hell you want."

Charlotte didn't want to hear it. She took her lemonade and cookies outside and sat on the porch swing, her feet barely touching the floorboards. A pair of black-backed gulls landed on the grass a few feet away. The birds looked sideways at Charlotte, their red, glassy eyes focused on the cookies.

"I don't think so," said Charlotte. "These are mine. Get your own. Scoot!"

She jumped out of her seat to scare away the birds but they merely stepped back a few feet and continued to stare.

When she'd finished, Charlotte walked to the rear of the house. Beside Grandpa's work shed, stacked four high and three across, was a pile of wire lobster traps waiting to be repaired. Beside the traps, a mountain of lobster buoys waited to be repainted with the Hale family's signature yellow-and-red stripe design. Grandpa saved that kind of work for the winter, when fishing was slower.

Ben Hale had been a lobsterman since he was fourteen years old, when he'd learned the trade from his father. Back then they used to haul the traps up by hand. There were no electric winches on the old boats. According to Gram, in those days you could tell which lobstermen worked the hardest by the muscles in their arms. Her grandfather had had the biggest biceps in Rocky Harbor.

Charlotte's father fished for a while when he was younger. But after he and her mother got married they moved out to the central part of the state so that her mother could live closer to her own family. Her father took a job driving a forklift for a gardening supply company, moving pallets of potting soil and fertilizer onto the trucks that would deliver them to big box hardware stores.

After her parents got divorced, Grandpa wanted her father to move back to Rocky Harbor with her and Charles. He was getting older, and he wanted to leave his boat and his business to someone in the family. But her father insisted he didn't want to be a lobsterman.

Charlotte walked down to the shoreline. It was nearly high tide. Gentle waves lapped at the top of the steps that led to a small beach when the tide was out. She stepped out onto her grandparents' small dock. Grandpa's rowboat thumped against the side of the wooden platform. Lying on her stomach, Charlotte peered over the edge of the dock into the murky green water. The smell of tar and damp wood mingled with the cool, salty air coming off the water's surface.

Come all you sailormen, listen to me
I'll sing you a song of the fish in the sea . . .

A girl's voice, low and soft, echoed through the marsh grass. Charlotte recognized the sea shanty from the Rocky Harbor Town Fair last summer. The voice seemed far away.

Up jumps the eel with his slippery tail;
He climbs up aloft and reefs the top sail . . .

Charlotte turned to see if there was someone behind her, but she was alone. She looked up at the yard, but it was empty, too.

Up jumps the shark with nine rows of teeth!
You eat the dough boys and I'll eat the beef!

As the singing grew louder the little hairs on Charlotte's arms stiffened and tingled.

Up jumps the herring, king of the sea!
Come all ye fishes, now you follow me!

At the opposite end of the dock, Charlotte heard a faint splash, the sound a fish makes when it jumps out of the water. She snapped around to see what had made the noise and found a message scratched into the soft wood at the dock's end: FnD Mp

SpEtR! The letters were uneven, as if written by a small child. Some of them had been deeply gouged into the dock's surface; others were scarcely visible.

Charlotte was sure the message hadn't been there a few moments before. She touched the letters with her fingers. The wood surrounding the carving was dark with water.

A few stray gulls called in the distance. The neighbor's German Shepherd yelped from his kennel next door, but the water around her was still.

"What the heck is that supposed to mean?" Charlotte said out loud. And who could have sneaked up onto the dock and scratched the letters into the wood without her seeing them?

The screen door on her grandparents' porch door swung open. Charlotte looked up and saw Grandpa coming across the lawn.

"Gram just made strawberry shortcake—got the berries from Blake Farm this morning," he said. "Come on in and we'll have ourselves a game of Rook."

Chapter 3

Charlotte was so surprised by the size of Marie Bouchard's house that it took her a few minutes to work up the courage to ring the doorbell. Mrs. B. lived in a historic sea captain's mansion on the cove, one of the biggest houses in Rocky Harbor. And although it was only a few blocks away from her grandparents' house, Mrs. Bouchard's neighborhood was like a different world.

Several houses just like Mrs. Bouchard's lined the street, each of them with bright flower beds lining their driveways. Majestic oak trees shaded their backyards from the hot afternoon sun.

The iron gate squeaked as Charlotte pushed it open. She climbed the worn granite steps, and just as she was about to press the bell, Mrs. B. came from around the side of the house, a pair of pink gardening gloves dangling from her left hand.

"Charlotte!" she said, "I'm glad you made it. Ezra's out back."

Charlotte followed her to the backyard. The house's slate roof was topped by a widow's walk, a small railed platform once used by sailors' wives to scan the horizon for their husbands' ships. The rear lawn rambled right down to the edge of the cove, offering a spectacular view of the water. A white gazebo stood at the back of the property, overlooking a wooden boat dock that bobbed quietly on the waves.

As if Mrs. Bouchard knew what Charlotte was thinking, she said, "This house belonged to my late husband René's family. They were ship builders who came here from the St. Lawrence River in Quebec many years ago. Their workshop was in that long building over there behind the carriage house. There's still a boat ramp in the back that leads down to the cove."

A boy, about fourteen years old Charlotte guessed, was standing near the top of a ladder by the main house. He was scooping clumps of decomposed leaves out of one of the gutters, his right hand covered by a yellow rubber glove.

"Ezra! We have a visitor!" Mrs. Bouchard hollered.

Ezra waved and began to climb down.

"Have a seat in the summer house," said Mrs. Bouchard to Charlotte. "I'll get you two something to drink."

It took Charlotte a moment to realize that "summer house" meant the gazebo. She sat down on a bench facing the water.

"Hi, I'm Ezra."

The boy stretched his hand through the open space in the side of the gazebo. At first, Charlotte didn't realize that he wanted her to shake it. She'd never met anyone even close to her age who had introduced themselves by shaking hands.

"I'm Charlotte—nice to meet you."

The boy smelled like laundry detergent and decaying leaves.

"I'll be right back. I just need to clean up."

Charlotte watched as Ezra walked across the yard to the carriage house and turned on the faucet for the garden hose. He had sandy blonde hair and was tall, well over six feet—much taller than her father. He rinsed his hands and forearms under the running water and wiped them dry on his khaki shorts.

On the gazebo table was a copy of *Moby Dick*. Charlotte picked it up and scanned the back cover.

"Have you read it?" Ezra sat down opposite her. He was all elbows and knees, his legs nearly too long to fit into the small space between the bench and table. "Summer reading. I started it yesterday," he said.

"No," said Charlotte. "But my Gram has a cat named Melville. This is her favorite book."

"That's cool," said Ezra, leaning back to try to get more comfortable. "So my grandmother invited you over here, huh? Don't feel like you have to stay. She's just really worried about me not having any friends."

"Why do you think I don't want to stay?"

"Because it's kind of awkward. Besides, a girl like you—you must have your own friends to hang out with."

15

"I don't, actually. I just got here a couple of days ago. You're the only person I've met so far.

"So, where do you live?" said Charlotte, changing the subject.

"Up in New Hampshire—near Lake Winnipesaukee. It's where my mom grew up. She owns a country store—she sells a lot of T-shirts and maple syrup to the tourists. My dad died a couple of years ago."

Ezra's navy blue polo shirt hung from his thin frame like an empty shopping bag. His angular nose and chin, which would have looked fine on an adult man, seemed a bit too large for his face.

"Oh, I'm sorry," said Charlotte. "I didn't know."

"No worries. I'm OK with talking about him. Where are you from?"

"I live out near Worcester," said Charlotte. "My dad grew up in Rocky Harbor though."

"Mine, too. I'm staying in his old bedroom. All his old Led Zeppelin posters and stuff are still up. Hey, do you want to go for a walk? It's kind of hot in here."

Charlotte followed Ezra to the edge of the lawn. They climbed down onto the thin strip of beach. The ground was wet and mucky and made a loud sucking noise each time one of them took a step.

"My grandfather and I used to dig for clams down here when I was a kid," said Ezra. "We had one of those metal rakes. I wonder if it's still in the carriage house? Hang on a sec."

Ezra scrambled back onto the lawn and took off running toward the large building beside the house. A few minutes later he returned with a short-handled clam rake and an aluminum pail. "You in the mood for some steamers?"

Charlotte watched as Ezra plunged the rake into the muck, opening up a wide hole.

"There's a ton of them down here! Check it out."

Charlotte crouched beside the hole and helped Ezra pluck the clams from the mud. After about twenty minutes the pail was full.

"Not bad," said Ezra. He brought the bucket down to the water's edge and filled it with seawater. Then he stuck his hand into the pail and gave the clams a stir. "This is how my grandfather used to do it. Got to rinse 'em off."

Ezra was rinsing the steamers for the second time when Charlotte saw something move out of the corner of her eye. Seated on the rocks lining the cove, just to the left of where they stood, was a girl about Charlotte's age. She had long, dark hair cascading over her shoulders in loose waves. Her skin was so pale that Charlotte couldn't imagine why she was out in the sun.

"Do you know her?" said Charlotte, pointing to the girl.

Ezra looked up from the bucket. "No. Maybe she's visiting next door." He raised his hand to wave.

Instead of waving back, the girl held up something shiny. The sun reflected off the object, creating a blinding glare that forced Charlotte and Ezra to shield their eyes. When they were able to look up again, the girl had disappeared.

"That was weird," said Charlotte. "Where'd she go?"

"Let's go see," said Ezra.

Leaving the clams to soak, they climbed across the slippery rocks, hand over foot, until they reached the spot where the girl had been sitting. There was no sign of her.

"She's just…gone," said Ezra. "I don't know how anyone could get off these rocks so fast."

"Look what she left behind." From between two rocks Charlotte pulled out a gold mirror, its glass about the size of an English muffin. It was heavy for its size, its metal frame cold to the touch.

"I think it's made from real gold," said Ezra, taking the mirror from Charlotte. Turning it over, Ezra revealed an intricate jeweled design. Blue sapphire dolphins and diamond-and-ruby flying fish flew across its back. The setting sun—or maybe it was the moon—had been made from iridescent mother-of-pearl.

"Why would she just leave this here?" said Charlotte. "It must be worth a lot of money. We should try to find her."

"We'll have to take it with us for now," said Ezra. "The tide's coming in."

Charlotte slid the mirror into the pocket of her shorts. They had almost made it back to the beach when a dark animal, about the size of a golden retriever, shot out from behind the rocks.

Charlotte screamed, nearly losing her balance and falling on the jagged boulders. Ezra reached out and grabbed her by the arm. The black beast had stopped in front of them, blocking their path.

Its eyes, like smooth discs, were the foul yellow hue of rotten cheese. A fishy odor wafted off its skin, forcing Charlotte and Ezra to cover their noses with their hands. It was identical to the animal Grandpa had hit on the day Charlotte arrived in town.

"What is it?" said Charlotte, hoping Ezra might be more familiar than she was with strange creatures living around the cove.

"Got me," he said, inching further away. "It sure smells bad though."

The creature let out a horrible growl. It bared a set of long, needle-like teeth, revealing its blood-red gums. Growling and hissing, the beast began moving toward Charlotte.

"Oh my God, it's after me!" Trying not to panic, Charlotte looked at the rocks behind her to see if she could climb to higher ground. She was trapped.

Frantically, Ezra looked around for a loose rock—anything he could use to fend the monster off. He lifted a slippery chunk of granite from a crevice between two larger rocks and prepared to hurl it at the creature, hoping to strike it in a spot that would slow it down.

Raising the rock over his head, Ezra aimed carefully for the space between the beast's eyes. But just as he was about to release it, another rock, even larger than the one he was holding, came flying at the creature from the direction of the water. Hitting its mark dead-on, the rock knocked the creature to the ground.

"Who threw that?" said Charlotte. "Is it dead?"

Ezra climbed down to where the creature lay. Foul smelling brown liquid oozed from the wound the rock had made. Pulling his shirt over his mouth and nose, Ezra nodded. "Looks dead to me."

Chapter 4

Ezra sat on the steps of the gazebo in his grandmother's back-yard, still shaken by the encounter with the horrible creature. Charlotte had gone home right afterward, leaving him to dump their bucket of clams back into the cove.

He watched as the water turned pink, then orange with the sunset. The sailboats near the horizon took on the colors of the sky so that everything looked as if it had been set ablaze.

Ezra walked to the edge of the lawn. The tide had come in and the water completely covered the stretch of muddy beach between the grass and waterline. The air smelled of salt and decaying reeds. A slight chill came up from the water.

The sky almost dark, Ezra picked up a flat stone and skipped it out over the cove. It bounced four times before sinking. He bent down to look for another rock, and felt something hard hit him on the head.

"Ouch! What the heck?" He stood up, rubbing the spot where the rock had struck him.

Ezra squinted in the dim light, trying to see who could have thrown it, but no one was there.

Finding another flat stone, Ezra skipped it, unable to see more than its first two bounces before it disappeared over the dark water. A few seconds later, he was hit by another rock, this time in the chest.

"Ahhh! Crap! Who's there? Come out and let me see you."

There was no reply. Frustrated, Ezra turned to go into the house and behind him he heard a girl laughing. It was a jolly laugh, like when someone hears a good joke. He stopped and turned around.

"Oh it's funny, is it? You'd better come out right now! I'm going in to call the police—little brats should be inside after dark."

Another rock whizzed by Ezra's head, landing on the lawn. Another pegged him in the shin, just below the knee. Soon rocks were flying, past his eyes and elbows, hitting him in the arms and neck. He was forced to run.

Just before he made it through the back door, Ezra heard a loud splash, like someone had jumped off the dock.

Nearly out of breath, Ezra stood with his back to the closed door. Blue-gray light from the television flickered on the walls of the living room where his grandmother sat. The house was quiet.

"Ezra? Is that you?" His grandmother called.

"Yep. Just me."

"One of your friends from home called. I left a message in Pepere's study."

Still dazed, Ezra walked down the long wood-paneled hallway to his grandfather's office. Pepere had died years ago, but his grandmother still kept the room exactly as he'd left it. Nautical maps from all over the world covered the walls. A mahogany bookcase against the far wall was crammed from top to bottom with moldering volumes covering every topic a seafarer might need to know about, from knot tying to shipbuilding. The hardwood floor was covered by a tattered Oriental rug.

Ezra sat in his grandfather's old swivel chair. Next to the telephone—a heavy, black rotary dial model—was a note in his grandmother's handwriting.

Dave called.

She could have just told me that, Ezra thought, rubbing a sore spot on his arm where a rock had hit him.

He was about to pick up the phone to call his friend back when one of the books caught his eye. Bound in black leather, it was a bit larger than the others. Ezra pulled it down and saw that it didn't have a title printed on its cover.

Ezra opened the book to its title page: *Accounts of Fantastic Maritime Creatures on Cape Ann.* The copyright date was 1905.

"Fantastic maritime creatures?" Ezra flipped to the middle of the book. He found an ink drawing of a creature that looked to be half bat and half fish. It had long teeth and was said to come after swimmers that ventured too close to its territory. The entry neglected to say where its territory was.

Another few pages in, he came to a chapter called "Mermaids, Water Sprites and Nymphs." According to the text, these were quite common on Cape Ann.

The book said that some people believed if they left gifts for the mermaids they would protect boats from storms, and help fishermen haul in big catches. People would leave all sorts of offerings on the rocks near the shore for them, from sardines and glass beads to silver spoons and candlesticks, which the mermaids were said to like because they were shiny.

On one page was a drawing of a man's lower leg. Just above the ankle was a sickle-shaped mark. The caption read: "Those who are descended from the sea people will bear a mark shaped like the crescent moon."

"What have you got there?" Ezra's grandmother came in carrying a plate of oatmeal cookies. "I thought you might like some of these."

"Thanks," said Ezra. "I was just looking at this old book."

"Your grandfather had that before we got married," she said. "I think it may have belonged to your great-grandfather." She walked behind the desk and looked at the book over Ezra's shoulder. "Ah, I always liked this one," she said, pointing to the text. "It's about a man who refused to leave a gift for the mermaids and got pebbles and shells thrown at him every time he went near the water."

Goosebumps formed on Ezra's neck and arms.

"Bring the plate back into the kitchen when you're done."

Chapter 5

Gram's wire shopping cart bounced behind her as Charlotte pulled it over the gnarled tree roots that crisscrossed the cement sidewalk. She'd offered to pull the cart for Gram, but now, with all the cars passing by, she wished she hadn't. More than that, she wished they could have taken the car instead.

An old-fashioned general store in Rocky Harbor's town center, Costa's Market had shadowy, narrow aisles lined with shelving that reached nearly to the ceiling. Colorful kites and Frisbees filled the racks near the checkout counter alongside crooked towers of beach pails and bins of rubber flip-flops. Bottles of sunscreen and bug spray crowded the shelves where sacks of rock salt and ice scrapers were displayed in the winter. The black-and-white checkerboard floor was worn almost clean through by the front door.

At the cash register Charlotte and her grandmother were met by a pimply teenager in need of a haircut. His white dress shirt was covered by a red apron with the name of the store embroidered on the front pocket.

"Hi, Mrs. Hale," said the boy as he scanned their first item. "Hot weather we've been having."

"Hello, Edward. This is my granddaughter, Charlotte. She's staying with us over the summer.

"Charlotte, this is Edward Kitchen. He helps us around the yard and shovels the snow. He's a great help."

Charlotte remembered Edward from when she was a little kid. His father, Bob Kitchen, was a line fisherman who was sometimes gone for days at a time. Gram used to watch Edward and his little brother, Timmy, while their mother was at work. Once, when she was five, Edward stole two dollars her mother had given her for the ice cream truck. He denied it, but she knew that he'd taken it, especially when he showed up the next day with a brand-new Matchbox car. She hoped he didn't remember her.

As Edward finished loading their bags into the wire cart, Charlotte heard someone calling her.

"Hey, Charlotte!"

Behind them, by an end-cap display of canned tomatoes, stood Ezra, a pricing gun in his right hand.

"I didn't know you worked here," said Charlotte.

"Just started yesterday. I figured I either get a job or spend the summer cleaning out my grandmother's gutters—at least this way I'll make some money.

"I was thinking of doing some exploring out on the rocks tomorrow when I get off work," Ezra said, "You want to come?"

"That sounds like fun," said Charlotte.

Across the street from Costa's, Charlotte and her grandmother stepped into Nathan Jacobs' fish market. Gram left the wire cart, now heavy with shopping bags, by the front door.

"Ava! How nice to see you. You look lovely as ever," Mr. Jacobs said.

He smiled as he reached into the gallon jar he kept behind the counter and pulled out a lollipop for Charlotte, not seeming to notice that she wasn't a little kid anymore.

"Just *look* at you, Charlotte. It seems like just the other day you were riding around town in your little blue stroller. I hope you're not getting too old for a treat?"

Gram and Mr. Jacobs talked while Charlotte stared out the window and watched the tourists, their arms loaded with packages and ice cream cones. She saw a couple of women go into Ocean Brothers' Antiques next door.

"Gram, is it OK if I go to the antiques store and look around?"

"Sure, honey. I'll come over when I'm done."

Set out on the sidewalk in front of Ocean Brothers' were wooden crates crammed with old books, stacked three and four high. Persian rugs, painted baskets, lamps, and other assorted knick-knacks had been neatly arranged on folding tables. A mahogany desk with carved lion's feet sat just to the right of the door.

Inside, the store was dark. Charlotte couldn't see a thing for the few moments it took her eyes to adjust. A violin concerto flowed from speakers hidden inside the walls. The shop smelled faintly of fish, something Charlotte assumed came from Mr. Jacobs' next door. The whole place reminded her of the attic of an old house, only fancier and less dusty.

The two women Charlotte had seen were in the back talking to a tall, oddly shaped man, his dark hair pulled back into a short ponytail. One of the women was holding a china platter upside down trying to read the maker's stamp.

Charlotte stopped at a table littered with picture frames, some with the photos still in them. She picked one up containing a black-and-white print of a young couple standing on the beach, their arms around one another's waists.

"Is there something I can help you with?"

Charlotte looked up to find the tall, hunched man that had been at the back of the store. He spoke with a heavy British accent.

"No, thanks. I'm just looking."

"That's what we're here for," said the man. "Sometimes you don't know what you're looking for until you see it."

Charlotte smiled, and hoped he would go away.

"I'm Morton Bathyal, the proprietor," the man offered. "Are you visiting? Such a lovely little town."

"No, I live here—well, my grandparents do. I'm staying with them for the summer. My grandmother's next door."

"Ah, yes," said Mr. Bathyal thoughtfully, "Nathan Jabcobs' market is quite popular." He circled around to the rear of the counter. "Since you live here, you may be interested in this."

He handed Charlotte a limp flyer.

The skin on his hand looked wet, as if he'd just run it under the faucet, but somehow the leaflet was dry.

"We're offering very fair prices," said Mr. Bathyal, pointing to the paper.

Charlotte read the first few lines:

Wanted:
Antique and Unusual Glass Bottles of All Kinds
Historic Maps, Especially of Local Origin

"Perhaps your grandmother has some old bottles around the house? You'd be surprised by the things people find in their very own homes."

"Maybe," said Charlotte, "I'll ask her."

"What would you say if I told you that fantastic and wonderful things could be lurking right beneath your nose?" Mr. Bathyal, who seemed unnaturally tall to Charlotte, leaned down so he could look into her eyes as he spoke. "Would you believe it?"

"Um, sure," said Charlotte, "but like I said, I'm just visiting."

Mr. Bathyal was quiet for a moment, his eyes locked on Charlotte's shoulder. He stretched out his right index finger, nearly touching the crescent-shaped brown birthmark just above her collar bone before he caught himself, jerking his hand away.

Charlotte, realizing what he was looking at, pulled the strap of her tank top over the mark. She was about to ask him what he thought he was doing when Mr. Bathyal spoke again.

"It seems there's something glowing in your pocket." He raised his eyebrows and pointed to Charlotte's shorts.

"Oh—yeah. That's my phone. My grandmother's probably calling me from next door. I should go. Thanks."

Charlotte hurried out the door, not sure why she'd felt the need to lie.

When she was out of Mr. Bathyal's sight she pulled the gold mirror that she and Ezra found on the rocks out of her pocket. She'd been carrying it around town whenever she went out in case she came across the girl who'd lost it.

26

Although the mirror's glass had been dark and cloudy when they'd found it, it was now glowing like the lens of a flashlight. In the center of the glow was the most hideous creature Charlotte had ever seen. The size and shape of a boa constrictor, red scales covered its body. Its mouth was full of long, pointed fangs, and its eyes were the color of egg yolks—the same as the creature's that had attacked her and Ezra on the beach. The beast seemed to be staring right at her.

Surrounded by blackness, the monster appeared to be swimming, writhing back and forth until, without warning, it turned to face her and snapped its horrible jaws.

Charlotte shrieked; the mirror clattered to the sidewalk.

The precious object slid across the asphalt, coming to a stop right in front of Ocean Brothers' front door.

Alarmed, Charlotte hurried after it. But just as she was about to put the mirror back into her pocket, Mr. Bathyal appeared in the doorway. His eyes locked on it.

"Dropped something?" One shoulder slightly higher than the other, he looked even bigger and more crooked than he had in the store.

"I've got it, thanks," she said, making sure the mirror was tucked safely away.

"Very good. You forgot this." He handed her the flyer. "I do hope we'll be seeing each other again quite soon."

Chapter 6

Charlotte woke with a start. The sun was just beginning to peak over the horizon, her bedroom washed in a pink glow. She was drenched with sweat, her nightshirt plastered to her back, her pillowcase like a damp rag. She'd had a horrible dream.

Ever since her parents' divorce she'd been having nightmares, usually about school. In those dreams she would be taking a math test and every time she solved a problem another one would appear at the bottom of the page. There were just minutes left before the end of the exam, but she would never be able finish it—no matter how fast she worked—and even if she got all the problems she had completed right, she was still going to fail. Her throat would get tight and she'd have to gasp for air. The room would start to spin and her math teacher, Ms. Thorne, would let out a bone-chilling laugh. That's when she would wake up.

This dream was completely different.

Charlotte sat in an old wooden boat traveling along a body of murky water. She couldn't tell if she was on a lake or a river, or even the ocean, because the sky was so gray. She couldn't see the horizon. The dim light coming from the yellow moon made it possible to see only a few feet in front of her.

"I think I'd like to go home now, please," said Charlotte, trying not to panic. The driver turned around then, and she saw that it was Morton Bathyal from the antiques store. He shook his head from side-to-side and turned back to the task at hand.

Not knowing what else to do, Charlotte thought she might try to swim back to the opening of the tunnel, but when she looked over the side of the boat she saw that the water was teeming with red serpent-like creatures, like the one she had seen in the mirror. One of the monsters rose up out of the water and clamped its teeth around her arm, pulling her into the water.

When she woke up her arm was stinging.

Chapter 7

Charlotte and Ezra walked side-by-side along Water Street. Packs of shoppers and dog-walkers passed by on either side of them, forcing one of them to stand to the side every few seconds to make room on the sidewalk.

In the middle of the intersection of Water and Wharf Streets, they stood beneath a twisted elm tree growing on the traffic island. Its trunk was at least three feet in diameter.

"This is a weird place for a tree," said Ezra. He placed his hand on the trunk as they waited for the traffic light to change.

"It's the Rocky Harbor Elm. It's supposed to be over 400 years old—that's what Gram says anyway. It was here before the roads," said Charlotte.

When they got to Barnacle Bob's restaurant they ducked through a thin stand of maple saplings and climbed out onto the rocks. It was nearly lunchtime and the clam shack was packed. People dressed in shorts and T-shirts sat on wooden benches outside waiting for a free table.

"The last time I went exploring along the cove, I was 9 or 10," said Ezra, hopping down from a large rock. He offered his hand to Charlotte so that she could jump down beside him.

The sun beat down on Charlotte's back and neck as they jumped from one rounded boulder to the next. After about twenty minutes, they came to a white clapboard church set high on the bluff above them, its paint peeling off in strips. The chapel was only a bit larger than an average-size house.

"I remember this church from when I was little," said Charlotte. "I don't think it's used anymore."

They climbed the cliff and hoisted themselves up onto the long grass growing in the churchyard. Ezra was tall enough to see through one of the chapel's large windows.

"Anything in there?" said Charlotte.

"Just the pews and the pulpit—and lots of dust."

At the front of the building, wispy razor grass and snarls of pink beach roses choked the lawn. Queen Anne's Lace and black-eyed Susans grew up through cracks in the four granite steps leading to the chapel's front door.

"It looks haunted," said Charlotte. "It doesn't look like anyone's been here in years."

"No kidding," said Ezra. "Watch out for ticks."

Ezra sat down on the bottom step. The fieldstone foundation holding up the church was crumbling in places, leaving holes large enough for animals to get through.

"Hey, look," Charlotte tamped down the weeds growing in front of the church's weather-beaten, glass-covered sign. "It says *S Pet r.* St. Peter's—some of the letters are missing. It's weird, but those same letters were part of a message that someone carved into my grandparents' dock the other day."

"Really?" Ezra came over to look.

"Yeah, they were carved right into the wood, just the way they are here: *S Pet r.* There were other letters, too." Charlotte didn't mention the part about the message appearing suddenly.

"Why would someone want to write 'St. Peter's' on your dock? Especially misspelled like that?"

"It was probably just some kids," said Charlotte, hoping it was true.

They walked another half mile on the rocks, down to the Annisquam Peninsula, a nose-shaped bit of land that jutted out into the ocean at the mouth of the cove. Stopping in front of the abandoned Annisquam Fish Cannery, the only building on the peninsula, they sat down on the rocks.

"The cannery looks the same as when I was a kid," said Ezra. "Minus the chain-link fence. Back then you could still go inside."

"Have you been in there?" said Charlotte. "My gram used to work there when she first got out of high school, before she married Grandpa. She used to pack sardines."

"I went inside with my dad once when I was about 10," said Ezra. "It was kind of creepy—all the conveyor belts and carts were still there.

"You know, this spot where we're sitting—it's supposed to be the exact place where the mermaid brought Boyd Morgan after he jumped off of *Gertrude Chance*—before it got sucked into the whirlpool," Ezra said. "At least that's what my dad used to say. You know that story, right?"

"Your grandmother told it to me—on the bus ride up here a few weeks ago."

"That's right. I forgot," said Ezra. "They say the place where *Gertrude Chance* sank is right about there." Ezra pointed to a spot about 100 yards out into the water.

"Do you think it's true? The part about the mermaid? I mean, I believe that a ship sank here once, even the whirlpool, but mermaids are a bit much," said Charlotte.

"Hard to say. If I were with my friends back home, I'd say no way, but here with you, alone—I can tell you this: There was this old guy who used to live in town when my dad was a kid. He used to swear that he saw mermaids all the time. My dad said he used to scare all the kids in town because he'd tell them if they didn't behave he'd send the mermaids after them when they were swimming."

"That just sounds like a crazy old guy," said Charlotte.

"Yeah, a lot of people did think he was crazy. But one time my dad saw him out on the rocks by the cove—right near the downtown—he swore he saw him talking to a girl with a fish's tail. He only saw her for a second, but he said there was no doubt."

Chapter 8

Ben Hale, Charlotte's grandfather, unlocked the door to his work shed—an aging building behind the main house. Its yellow paint was faded almost to white from decades of sun and salt air. When he was a boy, Ben's father had used the shop to build dories during the long New England winters. He sold the small boats to the clammers and lobstermen who worked the Cape Ann coastline. The hidden crevices of the building's long main room were still stuck fast with sawdust.

Setting his coffee cup down on the tool bench, Ben ran his hand along the hull of the old wooden boat he'd been working on.

He'd been taking his time restoring it. Several of the planks along the main deck had been rotten. Most of the past winter had been spent rebuilding the wheelhouse.

The boat had a life-size image of a mermaid painted on its port side. Her gaze met the horizon as she pulled a comb through her red hair. The years, the wind and waves had worn the illustration thin, but anyone could tell what it was. She was beautiful, her long, silvery tail stretching out toward the bow.

When Ben was growing up, most of the town's boats had been painted this way.

Morning light poured through the workshop's cloudy windows, particles of dust dancing in its beams. Ben pulled a paint-covered kitchen chair up to his worktable and sipped his coffee.

"Grandpa?" Charlotte called through the door. "Grandma says you should come help her get some boxes down from the hall closet."

"Why don't you visit a minute first? Seems like I haven't seen much of you since you got here—now that you're all grown up and have things to do."

Charlotte slipped through the door and sat down. "I'm 13, Grandpa, not all grown up. What are you doing?"

Strewn across the worktable were several days' worth of newspapers, a deck of playing cards and a yellow legal pad with several pages torn out.

"Just thinking," he said. "I'm thinking I hope I get to sail this boat before I'm too old."

After Grandpa went inside, Charlotte went out to the dock. With her back to the morning sun, she sat down Indian-style, closed her eyes and took a deep breath. The calls of seagulls and the distant ringing of the bell buoy at the entrance to the harbor made her feel sleepy.

Melville, her grandmother's cat, hopped out onto the dock and rubbed his head against Charlotte's ankles. The sunny dock was one of his favorite places to sleep.

Suddenly, Melville stiffened, his claws gouging her bare shin.

"Ouch!" Charlotte yelped. "What did you do that for?"

The cat raced to the end of the dock, his back arched, the fur along his spine erect. He let out a howl—long and low—the way he did when Kayak, the neighbor's German Shepherd, broke out of his kennel and got into the yard.

"What the heck is the matter with you?" Charlotte reached over and scooped Melville up by his middle. But then she heard it, too.

When I was a young lad, I sailed with the rest
On a Liverpool packet bound out for the west!

It was that singing! Just like she'd heard the night she'd found the letters scratched into the dock. Melville crouched in the hollow of Charlotte's lap, growling.

She thought of running into the house, but she was too frightened to move. Cold fingers inched up her backbone, sending shivers down her arms and legs. Whatever was doing the singing was right behind her, and it was coming closer.

The next I remembers, I woke in de morn
On a three-sky'l yarder bound south round Cape Horn!
Thud!

Something wet, heavy and rock-solid landed with a splatter on the dock next to Charlotte. The shock slammed the rowboat against the side of the dock, creating a splash that soaked Charlotte's sneakers and shorts. She covered her face with both hands. Something slick and cold, like the skin of a frog, brushed against her shoulder.

"Why don't you open your eyes?" Whatever was on the dock beside her knew how to talk.

Charlotte slid her fingers away from her face. Next to her was a girl, perhaps a little older than she was. In place of legs she had a fish's tail.

"Ahhhh! Oh my God!" Charlotte skittered to the far end of the dock, on all fours like a spider crab, until she was as far away as she could get from the mermaid.

The mermaid reached over and covered Charlotte's mouth with her cold, moist hand. "Shhhh. Do you want everyone to know I'm here?"

"You're real?" said Charlotte.

"Do I look real?" asked the mermaid, frowning.

She looked a lot like the painting on the side of Grandpa's boat, except her hair was pale yellow with a few streaks of bottle green. Her eyes were the color of the North Atlantic on a stormy day.

The end of the mermaid's tail hung over the side of the dock. She stirred the water with it, flicking it back-and-forth the way a nervous person bounces on his heels. The scales on her tail reflected the sunlight like tiny mirrors.

"What's the matter with you? You look like you've seen a red eel," said the mermaid.

"A red eel?" Charlotte still hadn't ruled out running into the house.

"Don't worry," said the mermaid. "If one of those stinking monsters tries to get near you I'll tear it in two!" She let out a snarl, raising her upper lip to reveal a row of pointed, white teeth.

"Anyway, they're only red when they're under water. They turn black, and get even uglier, on land."

Dropping her hands to her waist, the mermaid said, "Did you get my message? We really need to get going on this thing."

Her slender wrists were heavy with gold and silver bangles and bits of fishing line threaded with shells and plastic beads. She wore a necklace made of brass-colored bottle caps and chunks of smooth sea glass strung on a wire.

"Your message?" Charlotte asked.

"Yes. My message. On the dock. It's still here, see?" The mermaid pointed to the letters scratched into the wood.

"That was you?" asked Charlotte.

"No, it was a giant squid," said the mermaid. "Of course it was me. How many sea people do you think can read and write in English? I'm exceptional, you know. I learned from Captain Josiah Hale. He lived right here in this house."

"He was my great-great grandfather," said Charlotte, astonished. "He's been dead for 100 years."

"Pity, isn't it?" said the mermaid. "As soon as you people left the sea your life expectancy dropped dramatically. It was a mistake if you ask me. What's so great about legs anyway?"

Suddenly, the mermaid shot one of her slender arms down into the water and pulled out a fat, green crab, its legs wriggling. Grasping it by the back of its shell, she took a bite out of its thorax and chewed it into a pulp, shell and all. A thick liquid, like brown cottage cheese, dripped down her arm and from the corners of her mouth.

Charlotte, looking at the mess, swallowed hard. "What did you say?"

The mermaid let out a sigh. "And here I was thinking this was going to be easy." She reached over and grabbed the collar of Charlotte's T-shirt, green algae growing under her fingernails. Pulling the shirt down over Charlotte's left shoulder, she revealed her crescent-shaped birthmark.

"That," said the mermaid, "is what. You and your family used to be like us—with fins and sharp teeth, swimming around in the cove. And, believe it or not, it means that you—even though you don't seem very bright—are special. You're not exceptional like me, of course, but you should know that I don't waste my time talking to just any old land dweller."

"How did you know about my birthmark?" said Charlotte. "And what do you mean 'we' used to be sea people? And what's this about the message you left—which isn't actually a message, by the way. It's just a bunch of letters that don't spell anything."

The mermaid glared at Charlotte as she snapped up the rest of the crab in two bites, tossing the last bit of its shell back into the water. Looking over each of her shoulders, she lowered her voice to a hoarse whisper, "Well, look who's so smart. Why do you think my sister gave you that mirror? For fun? I'll have you know that the message says 'Find the map at Saint Peter's.' I spelled it exactly the way it is on the church sign. I had one of the seagulls go and look for me."

"The girl that lost the mirror is . . ." Charlotte stopped in mid-sentence, "What do you mean you had a seagull look at it for you?"

"All right, listen," said the mermaid. "It's not like this was my idea or anything, trust me. If I had my way I'd grow legs and take care of it myself. But, unfortunately, it doesn't work that way. Do you know about the blue bottle? Please say yes."

"Yes."

"Thank goodness," said the mermaid. "Do you remember the part about Boyd Morgan hiding the bottle? How he drew a map to show where he had put it? Well, you need to find it."

"The map?"

"The map, and then the bottle."

"But why?"

"Why? Now you want to know why?"

The mermaid began to raise her voice and then stopped herself. She took a deep breath to steady her nerves. "You need to find the blue bottle and deliver it to Oceanus before his evil brother gets his oily hands on it. He's here, you know. In Rocky Harbor running some kind of junk store. He's been looking for that bottle for a thousand years. He knows he's close to finding it—and if he does find it, we're all in serious trouble. This whole town will come crashing down into the sea in an explosion of fire and brimstone."

"Fire and brimstone?"

"OK, maybe not brimstone, but certainly fire—maybe even a volcano," said the mermaid.

"Why me?" said Charlotte finally. "I'm not good at things like this. I barely made it out of the seventh grade. And besides, no one's even seen the thing for three-hundred years. Who knows if it's still here? It could have gone out with the trash back in 1860."

The mermaid's eyes softened, and for a moment Charlotte thought she recognized something in her face. "You have to do it," she said, "because you're the only one who can. You're one of the only sea people left living on land in Rocky Harbor. No one else can use the mirror. We're depending on you."

The mermaid leaned in closer to Charlotte. Her skin was so pale that Charlotte could make out each of the violet-blue veins along her arms. "The map is hidden someplace in St. Peter's church. That's the reason I left you the message. You need to go there and find it without letting on to any of Mortimer's eels that you know something. They're curious about you. My sister killed one that had been following you the day she left you the mirror."

"Those horrible things are eels? They don't look anything like eels."

"They can take many forms," said the mermaid. "In the water they're red serpents. On land they look like the black monster you saw—or sometimes they take on the shape of humans. The only sure way to tell is the smell."

Charlotte nodded, remembering the repulsive odor of the dying creature.

"After you find the map, you'll have to use it to find the bottle. If you need to get in touch with me use the mirror. And when you find the bottle let me know right away."

"But what if I can't do it? Like I said, I don't exactly think I'm the best person to ..."

"If you don't find it before Mortimer does, Oceanus will make good on the promise he made to Boyd Morgan. Rocky Harbor will be destroyed along with everyone in it—and that includes sea people."

Barely making a splash, the mermaid slipped back into the cove.

"Wait! Don't go!" said Charlotte. "Where do I look for the map when I get inside the church? How do I use the mirror to talk to you? I don't even know your name."

The mermaid's head popped up on the opposite side of the dock. "My name is Eucla. If you need me just look into the mirror, or the surface of the water, and call my name. You're on your own with the map."

Eucla's head disappeared. Tiny bubbles rose to the surface.

"Charlotte? Are you out here?" Charlotte's grandfather walked across the lawn. "I thought I heard you talking to someone."

"Just talking to myself," said Charlotte, realizing afterward how stupid she sounded.

"How'd the dock get so wet?"

"Uh—I thought I saw a hermit crab. I was trying to catch it."

"Well, come and dry off. Your dad's on the phone."

Chapter 9

Water squished between Charlotte's toes as she walked across the lawn in her wet sneakers. When she got to the kitchen her grandmother was standing by the sink with the phone receiver to her ear.

"Here she is, Ethan. Hang on." She handed the phone to Charlotte, covering the mouthpiece with her palm. "Your dad has something he wants to talk to you about."

"Hi, Daddy." Charlotte sat down at the kitchen table. Her grandmother set a glass of cold milk in front of her and went out to the porch.

"Hi, Sugar. How are things going? I heard you've been having some good beach weather."

"It's been pretty nice," said Charlotte. "I like my room. I haven't been to the beach yet though."

"Well, sweetheart, I called because I have something I need to tell you."

"What is it?"

Her father hesitated, "You know Diane? The woman I've been dating?"

"Yeah, I remember her."

Charlotte's grandfather referred to Diane as "the barfly" because her father had met her playing darts at the neighborhood watering hole.

"She's going to be your new stepmother. We're getting married. Isn't that exciting? Her daughter, Chloe, will be living with us, too. In fact, they're moving in this weekend."

Charlotte knew Chloe from school. She was a year older, and would be entering her freshman year of high school in the fall. She always wore jeans that were two sizes too small and was constantly getting busted for smoking cigarettes behind the cafeteria Dumpster. She practically lived in the principal's office.

"But where's Chloe going to sleep? We don't have an extra bedroom."

"For now she's going to stay in your room, honey. Hopefully we'll be able to move to a bigger place soon."

Charlotte pictured Chloe going through the drawers in her nightstand.

"But you can't do that! I don't want her in my room! What about my stuff? What if she reads my diary? What about my desk and art supplies? And my jewelry and clothes. I don't want her touching them!"

"I'm sure she won't do anything like that, Charlotte. Chloe's a nice girl. Try to remember this is going to be an adjustment for her, too."

"What about Charles? What does he say about this?" She couldn't imagine her brother agreeing to live with Diane and Chloe without putting up a fight.

"We told Charles last night. So far he hasn't said much, but you know how he is."

Charlotte slammed the telephone receiver into its cradle on the wall.

In her room, Charlotte kicked off her wet shoes. They landed on the floor one after the other with a thud. She pulled off her damp shorts and T-shirt, tossed them in the corner, and crawled into bed.

The pillowcase was fresh and cool and smelled like fabric softener. Charlotte buried her face in it, trying to muffle the sound of her sobbing.

After a few minutes there was a knock on the door. "Charlotte, it's Gram. Do you want to talk?"

Charlotte lifted her head from the pillow. "No thanks. Maybe later."

"OK. I'll be downstairs if you need me."

Charlotte waited until her grandmother's footsteps faded away before setting her head back down. She stared at the cracks in the ceiling and tried to form recognizable shapes from them. She found one that looked like France and felt her eyelids getting heavy.

When she woke up she heard the banging of Grandpa's hammer in the work shed. The murmur of afternoon soap operas drifted up the stairway from Gram's kitchen television.

Too many bad, strange things had been happening since she'd come to Rocky Harbor. Charlotte wished she could go home. Not back to the duplex where she and Charles lived with their father—and soon with Diane and Chloe, but home like when she was little, with her mother and father sitting together on the porch after dinner while she and Charles ate Popsicles and zipped around on their scooters in the driveway.

It was on Easter, almost three months ago, that Charlotte had last seen her mother. And even on that day, her mother had spent all her time in the kitchen, and waiting on Bill, her stepfather, and his three boys.

She rolled over to face the wall and decided the best thing to do would be to leave Rocky Harbor. Even if the mermaid she'd met had been real, it simply wasn't possible that Rocky Harbor would fall into the sea if she didn't find some old bottle, any more than the rabid animal she'd seen on the rocks was really an eel, or the British man at the antiques store was a banished sea god, even if he did look like the hunchback of Atlantis. And on the off chance that those things really were true, she didn't see how any of them were her problem. She had her own life to worry about.

Charlotte loved her grandparents, but their house wasn't her home. It wasn't where she belonged.

Chapter 10

Morton Bathyal closed the door to the Rocky Harbor Maritime Museum behind him and stepped out onto White Pier. The staff hadn't been as helpful as he'd hoped. With their huge collection of maritime antiques and items recovered from shipwrecks, he'd had high hopes of finding the blue bottle on display, or at least discovering it was in their collection.

White Pier was bustling. Lobstermen loaded the day's catch into the beds of waiting pickup trucks while a sea kayak instructor offered pointers to a group of first-timers. Visitors roamed the pier with cameras, snapping photos of the brightly painted dories some of the fishermen used to get out to their boats in the harbor.

Near the pier's Water Street entrance was the Rocky Harbor Fishermen's Co-op, where fishermen and lobstermen sold their catches and bought bait and traps. The Gull Tavern, where fishermen drank beer and played darts after long days out on the water, was next door.

At the very end of the pier was the Rocky Harbor Maritime Museum. Constructed from the old harbor master's office, it was a favorite stop for summertime visitors. On rainy days many of the tourists roaming the downtown shops wore sweatshirts with the museum's mermaid logo on them.

It had taken Morton Bathyal several human lifetimes to devise an escape from his prison on the ocean floor. Trapped as he was in the darkness, his resources had been limited. In order to turn himself into a human, capable of living and breathing on the surface, he'd tried a variety of potions and spells. Finally, with the help of the red eels, he discovered devil's-apron.

A type of black kelp that grows near the surface of the Atlantic, devil's-apron was so powerful it could change Mortimer into a human man for five days when eaten in the right amount. In smaller quantities, the seaweed made it possible for red eels to live on land, too, though they didn't much resemble eels in their terrestrial state. With enough devil's-apron, a red eel could even take on human form. And though he wasn't very good looking, or fresh smelling, this is what Mortimer had done with his assistant, Anguilla.

Bathyal had to carry a constant supply of the plant. If its effects wore off he would change back into the gruesome bottom-dwelling creature whose form his brother had forced on him, unable to survive more than a few minutes on land.

Narrowing the blue bottle's location to Rocky Harbor had taken Mortimer decades. For fifty years he'd been posing as an antiques dealer in coastal towns up and down the Eastern seaboard of North America. He went from town to town, doing research and collecting old glass bottles.

Bathyal had had a stroke of good luck when a customer in Maine sold him a tattered sea captain's diary containing the story of the wreck of the *Gertrude Chance*. He knew then that he'd finally found the place he'd been looking for.

The problem, of course, was that the wreck was so long ago. No one living would have any idea where the blue bottle was, if it even was still in Rocky Harbor. His only chance, besides finding the bottle by accident, was to find the map drawn by the sailor Boyd Morgan showing where the bottle was hidden.

But paper didn't survive very long. And there was a good chance the map had been destroyed. And even if it hadn't, Bathyal had no idea how he was going to go about looking for it—that was until a human girl bearing the mark of a sea person had come into his shop with a mermaid's looking glass.

It was so simple that he couldn't imagine why he hadn't thought of it before. The water surrounding Rocky Harbor was full of sea people. They were the ones who saved Boyd Morgan and the blue bottle from the whirlpool, and they had been there when he had hidden the bottle.

Anguilla was waiting for Bathyal outside the museum. In his natural form a red eel, Anguilla had been Mortimer's constant companion since he'd been banished to the ocean floor.

Living on land was fine with Anguilla. He enjoyed seeing new places and all the strange animals and plants. But because he was used to living in total darkness, he was very sensitive to light. He wore black clothes and dark sunglasses for protection from the sun's rays. And even after eating a double portion of devil's-apron, Anguilla was never as convincing in his human form as Mortimer was. His skin and hair always gave off a rotten, fishy smell. And no matter how he tried, he simply could not get dry.

"No luck, Anguilla," said Mortimer. "I'm beginning to wonder if this bottle still exists. Did you find any information on that girl?"

"Her name is Charlotte Hale." Anguilla's throat began to fill with seawater, his words garbled. His devil's-apron was wearing off.

Mortimer sat down on a wooden bench in the shade beside the museum and motioned for Anguilla to sit next to him. Anguilla's shirtsleeve had ridden up to the middle of his forearm, exposing the tattoo-like image of a red eel that circled his wrist. The eel writhed and swam, as if it were alive.

"Cover up, *please*," said Mortimer, pulling down Anguilla's sleeve. We aren't going to make many friends here if you don't start presenting yourself…in a better light."

Bathyal took a deep breath and continued. "I want you to watch this Hale girl. Send a few of your eels to her house. Have them follow her around town. If we're lucky she might lead us right to the map, or even to the bottle itself."

He removed a leathery square of devil's-apron from the sharkskin bag around his waist. He was about to eat it when a clump of rockweed came flying up from the harbor, hitting him square in the back of the head. He spun around in time to catch two dark-haired mermaids stick their tongues out at him before they disappeared beneath the water.

"They know we're here," said Anguilla. "Soon Oceanus will know, too."

Mortimer bit off a chunk of the dried seaweed and chewed it. "In that case we must hurry. Here, eat this," he handed Anguilla the rest of the devil's-apron. "You're looking a bit damp around the edges."

Chapter 11

Gram sat at the kitchen table cleaning a bowl of green beans. *One Life to Live* was on. She was staring at the screen, a bean dangling from her hand, when Charlotte came down from her bedroom.

"Hi, Gram."

Gram dropped the bean back into the bowl. "Do you want something cold to drink? It must be ten degrees hotter up in that room."

"I can get it." Charlotte took a glass from the cupboard and filled it with water from the tap. She took a long drink, surprised by how thirsty she was.

Leaning against the counter, Charlotte said, "Gram, I've been thinking. Do you think I could have money for a bus ticket? I want to go visit my mom. I want to ask her if I can live with her and Bill—after this summer I mean."

Gram let out a sigh. "Charlotte, I know you're upset about what your father told you on the phone—Grandpa and I aren't exactly thrilled. And I know you miss your mother, but I don't think going to see her is such a good idea, especially unannounced. You know how busy she is with the boys. Why don't you call her and talk about it instead?"

After helping Gram with the dinner dishes Charlotte dug the flyer that Morton Bathyal had given her out of the desk drawer in her room. It had a few holes in it where fold lines had weakened the paper but she was still able to read it.

Wanted:
Antique and Unusual Glass Bottles of All Kinds
Historic Maps, Especially of Local Origin

Morton Bathyal had said he was offering "fair prices." If Charlotte could gather up enough old bottles she might be able to get the money to buy a bus ticket to Acton.

When her grandparents had settled down in front of *Wheel of Fortune* in the living room, Charlotte opened the cellar door and crept down the stairs one step at a time, as quietly as she could manage. Gram kept a lot of old stuff in the basement. There were bound to be at least a few bottles.

The cellar air was cool and smelled like overturned dirt. Dusty cobwebs crisscrossed the panes of the small windows set high into the walls. Beneath one window was a heap of ancient cardboard cartons labeled "Rocky Harbor Canned Sea Products. New England's Finest!"

In the carton on top of the pile Charlotte found several shoeboxes full of photographs and postcards. She came across a picture of her father by the cove, holding a fishing pole. He was wearing a pair of red running shorts and had long feathered hair and a slim mustache.

Charlotte was about to give up and go back upstairs when something near the ceiling caught her eye.

Set on top of the house's main support beam was an entire row of bottles, covered in dust. Charlotte pulled down a green hex-shaped flask only a couple of inches tall. She stuffed the old medicine bottle into her pocket and began taking down the rest of the bottles. She arranged them according to size on the dirt floor and looked around for something to put them in.

She found a pile of musty shopping bags—the kind with string handles that department stores used to give away at Christmas. Choosing one that looked sturdy, she began loading the bottles into it, trying to keep the clinking noises to a minimum.

Suddenly, unable to cope with the dust, Charlotte sneezed. The bottle in her hand went skidding across the dirt floor, coming to a stop when it smashed against the stone foundation.

The cellar door creaked open. "Charlotte? Are you down here?" Grandpa hesitated a moment before he was satisfied that the basement was empty and walked back to the living room.

Charlotte felt another sneeze coming on, the inside of her nose tingling. She squeezed her eyes shut and buried her face in her sleeve. She had no idea how she would explain what she was doing if one of her grandparents caught her.

The next morning, while Grandpa was out in the work shed and Gram was at a doctor's appointment, Charlotte brought the bag of old bottles up from the basement. In the bathroom sink she washed each one carefully before packing them all into her backpack. She left a note for Gram saying she had gone to the store, tossed her backpack over her shoulder and set off for Ocean Brothers'.

Morton Bathyal's shop looked much the same as it had the first time Charlotte was there. A few of the displays had been changed, but the same violin concerto drifted through the speakers in the walls. The shop still smelled faintly of low tide.

Charlotte rang the bell at the front counter.

After a few moments, an unusual-looking man appeared, dressed head-to-foot in black. He wore a long-sleeve, button-down shirt even though the thermometer out front registered over 80 degrees. His hands and face were as pale as winter moonlight.

"Can I help you?" said the man. "I'm Mr. Anguilla, the store manager."

Charlotte fought the urge to cover her nose. Trying not to breathe too deeply, she said, "I have a few old bottles I'd like to sell, please. The last time I was here the man told me you were looking for some." She handed Anguilla the flyer.

Hardly believing his luck, Anguilla was thrilled that Charlotte had walked into the store with a bag of old bottles. "Very good," he said. "Let's see what you have."

A chorus of sharp clinks erupted from her backpack as Charlotte lifted it onto the counter. One by one, Anguilla removed the bottles and examined them, lining them up in a row by the cash register. When he had taken the last one from the bag and set it down, he said, "Let me get Mr. Bathyal so he can give you a price."

Charlotte turned to look at the door every time someone passed by on the sidewalk. She hoped Mr. Jacobs from the fish store next door wouldn't decide to come in and browse. He'd be sure to tell Gram he'd seen her. She slipped on her sunglasses.

Finally, Mr. Bathyal appeared. "Ah, Miss Hale. How nice to see you again. Mr. Anguilla tells me you have some lovely old bottles for sale?" He picked up a large brown medicine bottle and looked at the stamp on the bottom. Searching the rest of the lot, he came across a small bottle made of pale blue glass.

"This is quite nice," he said. "Where did you say you found these?"

"They were just lying around the house," said Charlotte.

Bathyal examined the blue bottle further, turning it over in his hands before setting it back down. "I'll give you forty dollars for the lot."

Charlotte nodded in agreement. Forty dollars was more than she'd expected. It was more than enough money for a bus ticket. She'd have money left over for lunch.

Mr. Bathyal handed her two crisp $20 bills. Before she could say anything else, he began loading the bottles into a cardboard box. "Have a lovely day. Please come back and see us again."

With the money in her pocket, Charlotte walked across the street to Costa's Market.

She felt her muscles relax as she entered the air-conditioned store. The market sold bus tickets at the customer service counter, along with lottery scratch cards and cell phone vouchers. She waited while Mr. Costa helped another customer.

But before Mr. Costa had finished, though, Ezra came out of the office door behind the counter. "Hi, Charlotte. I was thinking of giving you a call later. Are you shopping with your grand-mother?"

Charlotte had forgotten that Ezra worked there.

"Actually, I need to talk to Mr. Costa about something," she said. "Call me tonight if you want."

"OK. Sure thing. Talk to you later."

Chapter 12

Charlotte got up before dawn, the sky over the cove the color of a ripe peach. Her bus was scheduled to leave at 6:25 a.m. and she had to allow enough time to walk to the bus stop, almost two miles away. She had showered and packed the night before, so all she had to do was get dressed and brush her teeth.

She left a long note for her grandparents on the kitchen table. She hoped she wasn't going to hurt their feelings by leaving, and she didn't want them to worry, but they had to understand. Gram couldn't really expect her to live with Diane and Chloe.

The bus was nearly empty when Charlotte stepped on. It was just her, the driver and a college-age boy sitting in the back, headphones covering his ears.

With some of the money she had left over from buying the bus ticket, Charlotte bought a card for her mother. On the front it said "Thinking of You Mom." A photograph of two women, one older and one younger, with their arms around each other was under the headline. Charlotte pulled the card from her backpack along with a ballpoint pen and set to thinking about what she should write. After several minutes she wrote: *I can't wait to come live with you and Bill! I love you!*

Charlotte arrived at Boston's North Station, where she needed to change buses, at 7:50 a.m. She walked up and down the rows of parked buses, comparing the numbers painted on the wall near their parking spots to the number on her ticket until she found the right one.

Charlotte's second bus arrived in Acton, the depot not much more than a concrete platform next to the commuter train station, just past 9:00 a.m. Because it was Saturday only a few people were at the train station, and there was no one working in the ticket booth. A Vietnamese woman selling cut flowers gave Charlotte directions to her mother's house on Wimbley Street, just a few blocks away.

As Charlotte walked it occurred to her that her mother might not be home. She could be out grocery shopping or taking one of the boys to baseball practice. And what if they were away on vacation? She began to think maybe Gram had been right about calling.

Wimbley Street was long and winding and looked as if it had been freshly paved. Big new houses rose up behind smooth green lawns on both sides of the street. Although there was no traffic, Charlotte was careful to stay on the sidewalk. She wanted to look like she belonged there.

Finally, she reached number 563, her mother's house.

As Charlotte walked around to the side of the house she noticed a red Buick Regal parked in the driveway – just like Grandpa's car. She took out the card she'd gotten for her mother and climbed the steps.

Before Charlotte could knock, her mother was at the door. Charlotte opened her mouth to say hello, expecting a big hug.

"What the hell do you think you're doing here?" Her mother swung open the screen door with a bang, motioning for Charlotte to step into the kitchen. "What makes you think you can just show up? I had to cancel two appointments this afternoon, and I had to find a ride for Bill Jr. to get to his fencing lesson. It's a good thing your grandmother called me. I can just imagine what Bill would do if he came home to find you sitting on the porch."

Still clutching the card, tears welled up in Charlotte's eyes. The skin on her mother's face was pinched around her mouth and eyes, making her look years older than she was.

"But, Mom, I miss you. I just thought … maybe we could talk. I was thinking I might be able to come live with you in the fall …"

Her mother rolled her eyes. "Did your father put you up to this? I heard he's getting married again. Is that right? This is just like him, trying to get out of his responsibilities. I'd like to know when he's going to grow up and figure out that he's not the only person on the planet."

"No, Mom, it was my idea." Charlotte's voice was shaky. "Dad doesn't know I'm here. I just miss you. I want to live with you, like when I was little."

"Your father and I agreed on custody for you and your brother years ago. You tell him if he's interested in changing that he can call my lawyer."

Charlotte's mother left her standing alone in the kitchen, its shining stainless steel refrigerator humming in the corner. Through the window over the sink Charlotte saw a group of sparrows gathered at the birdfeeder. A package of chicken breasts had been set out to thaw on the kitchen counter.

On the computer desk at the far end of the room, framed school photographs of Bill's sons had been neatly arranged.

Charlotte heard the basement door open and her mother's voice calling down to the family room. "Eva, Ben, she's here. You can take her home now."

Chapter 13

Charlotte's grandparents said very little on the ride back to Rocky Harbor. Grandpa offered to stop at Friendly's for lunch, but Charlotte wasn't hungry. Someplace on I-95, about half way home, Charlotte cracked the window and slipped the card she had bought for her mother through the opening.

As the red Buick passed over the Rocky Harbor town line on Route 133, a long line of traffic came into view. Grandpa brought the car to a stop.

"Seems like a lot of beach traffic so late in the day," he said. He flipped through the radio dial looking for a traffic report.

Gram rolled down her window and stuck her head out. "I see blue lights. Must have been an accident."

After about 15 minutes the car began to inch forward. When they finally arrived at the scene of the trouble, Charlotte was astounded. Two massive boulders had come loose from the glacial rock formation on the side of the road. They blocked the entire eastbound lane of Route 133, as well as part of the westbound side. The larger of the two giant rocks, over ten feet tall and five feet across, cast a shadow across the road. A front loader had been called in to try to move the boulders, but it had so far managed only to push one of them far enough out of the westbound lane to allow one car to pass at a time.

Grandpa rolled down his window. "What happened, Al?" he asked one of the policemen.

"Earthquake," the officer replied, one hand resting on his slim hip. "Never seen anything like it. Half the town has no power. Came out of nowhere."

Grandpa drove slowly the rest of the way home, trying to avoid the downed power lines and tree branches that littered the road. The traffic light downtown was out, and in spots Charlotte noticed other boulders—in people's backyards and scattered along the shoreline—that had come loose from the bedrock that made up Cape Ann.

Grandpa and Gram's house looked fine when they pulled into the driveway. The oak tree in the backyard was still intact and the light was on in the workshop, meaning they hadn't lost power. When Charlotte got out of the car she peered down at the cove. A massive rock had broken free from the cliff near the waterline and had landed smack in the middle of her grandparents' small beach.

Up in her room, Charlotte lay down on the bed, too tired to cry. Her mother didn't want her. She was just going to have to get used to it.

The sound of waves splashing against the rocks outside lulled Charlotte to sleep.

"Hello, Charlotte! Hellooooo? Where are you?"

Charlotte woke with a start to the sound of someone shouting. She scrambled around the room, placing her ear to the floor and walls, overturning piles of laundry, trying to figure out where the voice was coming from.

"Oh, come on! I don't have all day! And neither do you! Have you *seen* what kind of shape Rocky Harbor is in? Where have you been?"

Finally, Charlotte unzipped the front pocket of her backpack and pulled out the gold mirror. The glass was glowing white and blaring like a loudspeaker.

"Hello?" said Charlotte, looking at the mirror. "Is someone talking to me?"

The watery image of a mermaid began to form in the cloudy glass.

"It's about time," Eucla said. "You left didn't you? You weren't going to come back. You are supposed to find the map. Oceanus is getting angry."

Charlotte took a deep breath "Well, yes. I did leave. I had something important I needed to do. Uh, how are you talking to me?"

"Something important? What could be more important than saving the town where you live? There's no way of telling when the next earthquake will be. And the next one just might knock that big tree in your grandparents' yard right onto the house. Splat!"

"Right," said Charlotte under her breath. "The thing is, I don't live here. And I still don't think I'm the right person for this job. I'm not good at anything. I never finish anything I start. My own mother doesn't even want me. You'd better find someone else."

"There is no one else!" Eucla yelled. "I thought we went over this already? If you don't do this, Charlotte, we're all doomed. That's all there is to it."

The mirror went dark in Charlotte's hand.

Taking a deep breath, Charlotte picked up the telephone beside her bed and dialed Ezra's number.

Chapter 14

Charlotte and Ezra scrambled along the rocks framing the cove. Although it was early in the day, the air was thick and humid, forcing them to move at half the speed they normally would.

"So you really think there's a map in the old church showing the spot where someone hid a bottle 300 years ago?" said Ezra, taking a swig from his water bottle.

"That's what Eucla says," said Charlotte. "We at least have to look."

She had spent almost an hour the day before telling Ezra about Eucla, the blue bottle, Morton Bathyal and the red eels. To her surprise, he didn't think she was nuts.

They made it to the small white church after about twenty minutes of clambering from one boulder to the next. Climbing the steep bluff, Ezra stomped down the waist-high grass, bending back scrubby sumac saplings to create a path. When they came to the front of the building, the sign was just as it had been the last time they were there.

"I don't think anyone else has been here," said Charlotte.

"I doubt it," said Ezra. "You can't even see this place from the main part of town. I asked my grandmother about it. She said this was Rocky Harbor's original church, from the 1600s. This used to be the town center. Now they don't even plow the road in the winter."

"I wonder who owns it?" said Charlotte, sitting down on the cool granite steps to rest. She had tucked the gold mirror safely into the front pocket of her backpack before she left her grandparents' house.

"I asked her that, too," said Ezra. "I guess it's owned by the town. Years ago they used to rent it out for weddings and things, but no one's used it in ages."

Ezra jimmied the handle on the front door. It was locked.

They went around to the side of the building and checked the rectangular windows cut into the foundation. One of them was open.

Slipping off his backpack, Ezra pushed the window frame inward, lifting it up on its hinge with a rusty squeak. "Look at that! Hand me my backpack after I get in, OK?"

Ezra slid through the narrow opening feet first with his stomach pressed against the sill. His legs were so long that his feet reached the basement's dirt floor while his head was still sticking out of the window. "Uh, I guess I can get my own backpack. I'll go around front and let you in."

Brushing away dust and cobwebs from the front of his shirt, Ezra reached into his pack and pulled out a flashlight.

The walls were lined with stacks of cobweb-coated chairs. To the far right of the window where Ezra had come in was a red door.

Just as he was about to turn the doorknob, he heard a noisy crash on the other side of the room.

Swallowing hard, Ezra closed his eyes and pressed his back against the door. He tried not to breathe. From the back of the cellar shuffling sounds grew louder and louder as whatever had made the noise came toward him.

After a few moments the noise stopped. Ezra summoned the courage to open his eyes. A fat raccoon sat on the floor in front of him. Her wide eyes reflected the flashlight's beam with an eerie green glow.

"You scared the hell out of me!" he said to the raccoon, catching his breath. The animal turned around and waddled back to the rear of the basement.

With the creature gone, Ezra tried the door again. Its hinges were corroded from years of exposure to the sea air. He leaned against it with all his weight, eventually creating an opening just wide enough to squeeze through.

In contrast to its basement, St. Peter's sanctuary was bright and pleasant. Sunlight streamed through the wide six-over-six windows. Dappled light, reflected off the surface of the cove, danced along the white walls. The pews had been covered with white sheets, giving the large space a ghostly feeling.

Ezra went to the narthex and unbolted the heavy oak door.

"Charlotte! Over here!"

She appeared from around the side of the building. "We have to be quiet. I just saw old Mr. Carson, Gram's neighbor, out walking his dogs." She slipped through the door. "If he finds out we're in here he'll call the cops for sure."

They sat down in one of the front pews.

"Wow. It's beautiful," said Charlotte. "You'd never imagine it, seeing the outside."

"So, where should we look first?" said Ezra, not wanting to waste time taking in the scenery. "The last thing we need is the cops showing up."

"It could be in here anywhere, I guess." Charlotte waved her hand to indicate the stacks of cloth-bound hymnals stored at the ends of the pews. "Maybe even in one of those books."

Erza frowned. "It will take all day to look through those. Didn't Eucla say anything else?"

Charlotte shook her head.

"OK," said Ezra. "Let's look around."

Walking up the steps to the pulpit, he checked the shelves underneath. "Nothing up here."

To the right of the pulpit was a door. The tin sign tacked to it had been painted over, but up close Charlotte could still make out what it said: STUDY.

"This was the minister's office," said Ezra. "I bet the map's in here." He tried the handle, but the door was locked. "Great. We get this far and now we're stuck."

"Maybe the key's around someplace," said Charlotte. "When I was a kid the church sexton used to have a big ring of keys, one for every door."

"I don't think there's a sexton here, Charlotte."

"No, but maybe there's a supply closet. Let's look in the back."

At the rear of the sanctuary was a set of double doors leading to a short hallway.

"Down here," said Charlotte, motioning for Ezra to follow her.

They tiptoed along the corridor until they came to a small kitchen. Inside was an avocado green electric stove, the kind that operates with push buttons instead of knobs. The countertops were bright orange. The calendar page tacked to the wall was from April 1975.

"This place needs a makeover," said Ezra, peeking inside a stainless steel coffee pot.

Charlotte opened one of the cabinets to find stacks of china plates, cups and saucers, and a large cut glass serving bowl. She opened a second cupboard full of cookbooks. "What do people at a little church like this need to cook?"

Ezra began opening drawers. Most of them were filled with silverware and cooking utensils. Then, in the last drawer, beneath several books of matches and a few crumbling receipts, he found a ring of keys. He held them up and gave them a shake. "Let's see if they work!"

Out in the hallway again, they came across another set of double doors, slightly ajar.

Ezra pushed them open with his foot. It was a large room, mostly empty and much darker than the sanctuary had been. Chairs and tables were stacked in irregular heaps against the back wall. The floor was made of polished hardwood.

"This looks like a function room," said Ezra, still holding the keys.

"There's a little stage," said Charlotte. "Maybe they used to have plays here, or music. Imagine how nice it would have been with all the windows open and the cove outside."

The stage was about twelve feet wide and had a blue velvet curtain hung across it. Charlotte pulled it aside.

Backstage were piles of cardboard boxes full of Christmas decorations and brittle magazines. A rolling wardrobe in the corner was jammed with zip-up garment bags. Everything was covered in a thick layer of dust.

Charlotte crept around the boxes and came to another door. "Ezra, come here. I need those keys."

The first two keys were too large for the lock.

"Try the one on the end," Ezra said. "The small one."

Charlotte slid the key into the lock and turned it.

"Cool!" she said, pushing open the door.

It was a small office, only a bit larger than Charlotte's closet at her grandparents' house. The only furniture was a mahogany roll-top desk and two chairs, both sitting on a braided wool rug. The light source was a small window on the far wall.

Ezra sat down and tried rolling up the top of the desk.

"It's stuck," he said.

"Let me try," said Charlotte. "My mom has a desk like this. The top is always getting stuck. You have to push one side at a time."

Charlotte pushed the desktop up on the left and then on the right until it rolled up into place.

"Look," said Charlotte, "a Bible."

In the center of the desktop was a Bible five inches thick at the spine and bound in white leather. Fancy gold lettering graced its front cover.

"This belongs at the pulpit," said Ezra. "Someone must have put it in here for safe keeping."

Ezra picked up the book. "My grandmother has a Bible kind of like this. Our family tree is in it." He cracked open the cover.

Red, gold and blue illuminations of birds and animals decorated the first book of Genesis.

"It looks like it was painted by hand," said Charlotte. "It's beautiful. But I don't see a map."

"You're right," said Ezra. "We should put it back."

Ezra placed the Bible back in the center of the desk and grasped the roll top.

"Wait. What's this?" Charlotte pointed to a discolored piece of paper, its edge barely visible among the Bible's pages.

Charlotte reopened the large book and removed a delicate piece of parchment.

"Ezra, I think this might be it," she said, unfolding the yellowed paper.

Ezra took the frail document and brought it over to the window. "It's hand drawn. The lines are pretty faint, but it looks like it could be Rocky Harbor. This church is on it, and the cove. Then there's what looks like a huge field next to a big tree."

"Let me see," said Charlotte. "That's the Rocky Harbor Elm. The one downtown. This field is where the downtown is now.

"Ezra, look at this!" said Charlotte.

In the lower left-hand corner of the map was a faded signature: *B. Morgan.*

"That's the guy who survived the wreck of *Gertrude Chance.* The one who hid the bottle," said Ezra.

"Ezra, I think this is his map."

"But it doesn't have anything about a bottle on it."

"Well no, but maybe we're missing something. We'll have to take it with us."

Charlotte rolled the map up inside a sheet of clean paper she found in a desk drawer, slipped a rubber band around it, and tucked it into her backpack. They returned the ring of keys to the kitchen and hurried back to the narthex on the far side of the sanctuary.

Ezra said, "Take my backpack and go out this door so I can lock it behind you. Meet me by the cellar window."

Charlotte waited on the side of the building, hoping that Mr. Carson and his pack of mongrel dogs had gone home. The map in her bag made her uneasy. If Eucla was right, and Charlotte was beginning to think she was, Morton Bathyal and his eels would do anything to get their hands on it.

The Blue Bottle

Beneath a slim maple tree on the opposite end of the churchyard, Charlotte thought she saw something move.

Shielding her eyes, she made out a dark shape beneath the
tree, like a shadow. It seemed to be moving toward her, crouched
in the tall grass. The rank smell of rotten fish floated on the
breeze.

Charlotte bent down to peer into the window, hoping to find
Ezra coming out. When she turned back around, the black shape
had moved closer. Now fewer than twelve feet away, its yellow
eyes glared at her through the brush.

When Ezra finally lifted the window, the creaking sound
make Charlotte jump.

"Ezra, there's something over there. In the grass. It's moving." Charlotte's back was pressed up against the white clap-
boards.

"It's probably just one of Mr. Carson's dogs," said Ezra. He
squatted down beside Charlotte. The creature's eyes, dead like a
shark's, met his.

"Holy crap! That's not a dog." Ezra tried not to raise his
voice. "Let's go." He grasped Charlotte's hand, pulling her
toward the front of the church. "We're taking the road back.
Forget climbing across the rocks."

Chapter 15

Charlotte took Boyd Morgan's map from her backpack. Spreading the delicate parchment out on her desk, she took out a clean sheet of paper and a pencil and began to copy it, doing her best not to leave out a single detail. If she was going to have to hunt for an old bottle with a bunch of sea monsters lurking around, she had to keep the original map safe.

When Charlotte got to the Rocky Harbor Elm she noticed a faded mark beside it she hadn't seen in the church. It was a tiny rectangle, about the size of a match head, just beneath the tree's trunk. Holding the paper up to the desk lamp, she saw that the rectangle had a much smaller, circular shape at the top. The bottle was hidden someplace near the tree!

Ezra squinted at Charlotte's drawing. "How do we know the bottle is still here? It could have been moved a hundred years ago."

"We'll just have to look," said Charlotte, poking her sneaker around the tree's trunk.

"It's not like we can stand here in the middle of the street digging a hole. Someone will call the cops—and that Mortimer guy's store is right over there. He might be watching us right now." Ezra sat down on the bench beneath the tree and mopped the sweat from his forehead with the hem of his shirt. The digital sign outside Cape Ann Savings Bank said it was 94 degrees.

Charlotte sat down next to him. "You're right. We need some kind of plan."

Downtown traffic whizzed past them. Ezra said, "Why don't you just come over to my house and we'll go swimming. It's too hot. Let's forget about this for now."

"OK, but I have to get my bathing suit." When she stood up from the bench, something up in the tree caught her eye. "It looks like the earthquake the other day widened that hole in the tree."

About twelve feet up, fresh wood was showing around the edges of a scar-covered knothole.

"I bet I can get up there," said Ezra.

He climbed on top of the park bench and grabbed onto a low branch, hoisting himself up into the elm.

"Can you see anything?"

"It's pretty dark inside. But it looks like something's in there. A box—made out of metal. I can't get it out because the tree's grown over it. The hole's too small." Ezra dropped back to the ground, landing on his feet. "I've got something in my back-pack." Rummaging through the black hiker's pack he always carried, Ezra pulled out a Swiss Army knife. "I got this for my birthday last year. It's got a saw."

As Ezra climbed back up the tree, Charlotte grew anxious. What if someone saw him and really did call the police? "Hurry, OK?"

"I'll go as fast as I can." Sawdust drifted down, covering the park bench in fine, coffee-colored powder.

"Stop!" Charlotte called. "Someone's coming." From across the street a couple with a toddler in a stroller came toward them. Charlotte smiled. They didn't even notice Ezra.

"OK, go," said Charlotte after they'd passed.

Ezra sawed furiously, trying to free the rusted metal contain-er. His arm ached. His knuckles scraped the rough bark causing them to crack and bleed.

After what seemed like an eternity, Ezra said, "I've got three sides done. I'm going to try getting it out."

He pushed as much of his right hand as he could into the hole. It was a tight squeeze, but he managed to wriggle the corroded box back-and-forth until it came right to the edge. He slipped the blade of his saw between the box and the tree, ready to pry it loose.

"Stop!" said Charlotte. In front of Ocean Brothers' Antiques, among the crates of moldering books and mismatched dishes, stood Morton Bathyal and Mr. Anguilla. They were looking right at them.

"Bathyal's watching us," said Charlotte.

"Let's hurry then," said Ezra, prying the box from the tree with a soft *pop*. "Got it!" Holding the box under his arm, he jumped down. As soon as his feet hit the ground he scooped up his backpack and stuffed the box inside.

"He's coming!" said Charlotte.

Ezra zipped his pack and brushed the sawdust from his shirt.

"Good afternoon," said Mr. Bathyal. "Lovely seeing you again, Ms. Hale. Those bottles you sold me were quite nice, but not exactly what I was looking for."

Ezra stood behind Charlotte, his hands behind his back in order to hide his bleeding knuckles.

"I couldn't help but notice you two under the tree," said Bathyal. "Quite romantic isn't it?"

Terrified he would look up and notice the freshly sawn hole, Charlotte said, "We were just about to leave. We're going swimming."

"Fine day for that," said Bathyal. His eyes wandered along the trunk of the tree and the ground beneath it. "Don't let me keep you—just thought I'd pop over and say hello."

"Thanks," said Charlotte. "Have a nice day."

Mr. Bathyal turned to leave. "Before I go, here's a flyer for your friend. We're always looking for new merchandise." He held out the paper to Ezra.

With no other choice, Ezra reached out to take the flyer, exposing his bleeding hand.

"Goodness," said Bathyal. "What ever happened?"

"I was working on my boat this morning," said Ezra.

"I see," said Mr. Bathyal. "You may want to get that attended to."

It was then Morton Bathyal looked up. His black eyes widened when they met the spot on the tree that had been opened by Ezra's saw.

Chapter 16

Charlotte and Ezra hurried down Water Street toward his grandmother's house.

"Do you think he knows?" asked Charlotte.

"He knows I was up in the tree. If he really is who you say he is, he's going to put two and two together eventually."

When they got to Mrs. Bouchard's house they sat down on the back porch. Screened in on three sides, a wicker sofa and chairs were set up along one wall, offering anyone who sat there a stunning view of the cove. Propped up in the corner was what was left of a ship's masthead—a woman, naked from the waist up, holding aloft a drawn sword. Her torso and face had been badly damaged by worms.

Ezra pulled the metal box from his backpack and set it down on the glass coffee table.

"I wonder how we get it open?" he said, brushing away the sawdust and crumbs of rust that had fallen away from its sides.

Charlotte reached over and picked up the box, shaking it. "It doesn't seem like there's anything in it. It feels too light."

"The bottle could be really small," said Ezra. "Or surrounded by padding. Let's take it to the carriage house. My Grandpa's old workbench is in there."

The carriage house's enormous doors had been built to allow horse-drawn carriages to pass through them. Charlotte could still smell the hay that had once filled the now empty horse stalls in the back.

Ezra set the box down on the wooden workbench. He considered the collection of tools hanging on the pegboard in front of him before choosing a hacksaw.

"Are you sure that's the right thing to use?" asked Charlotte.

"The lid is rusted shut. I doubt I'll be able to pry it open."

Holding the box with his left hand, Ezra began to saw through it, careful not to damage whatever might be inside. The fragile metal came apart after only a few strokes.

"That was pretty easy," said Charlotte. "What's inside? Can you see anything?"

Ezra pulled off the sawed end of the box. "Looks like a piece of paper."

Careful not to catch his skin on the jagged edges, Ezra reached inside and retrieved a folded piece of parchment.

"No bottle?" said Charlotte.

"Doesn't look that way." Ezra unfolded the paper and smoothed it out on the workbench.

"It looks like a poem," said Charlotte. "I don't get it. The tree was marked on the map. The bottle was supposed to be there."

"Read it," said Ezra.

The object you seek is small and sleek,
As blue as the summer sky
You won't find it here,
For Mortimer is near
To unlock the power of legends of old
Visit the house with windows of gold

"Great," said Charlotte. "Now we have to figure out what this means. Windows of gold? This note is probably 200 years old. How did the person who wrote it know about Mortimer?"

"Good question," said Ezra.

Charlotte left Ezra's house tired, and more than a little worried.

Rather than turning down Wharf Street toward her grandparents' house, at the last moment she decided to take a left onto Gloucester Street toward the cemetery. When they were younger, she and Charles used to go for walks there with her grandfather. It was one of her favorite places.

68

Set at the very end of Gloucester Street, The Rocky Harbor Burial Ground was surrounded by a ten-foot wrought iron fence. Some of the people interred there had been buried as long ago as the 1620s, their gravestones worn to the thickness of the Rocky Harbor telephone directory.

Charlotte wandered up and down the paths in the oldest part of the cemetery, taking time to read the names on the stones. Flocks of crows perched high in the surrounding oak trees cackled to one another. A few of the black birds swooped past Charlotte as the gravel pathway crunched beneath her feet.

Some of the stones Charlotte saw were broken in two; others had sunk partway into the ground. One in particular caught Charlotte's eye. Made of gray-blue slate, it was weather-worn and covered with patches of mustard-colored lichen. The name engraved on its front was Ruth Smith.

Charlotte wondered if it could be the Ruth Smith in Mrs. Bouchard's story.

On the back of the headstone was a faint engraving. When she got up close to it, Charlotte could see it was a mermaid, her elegant tail sweeping across the stone. Just below the image in small print was written: *Dearest Eucla.*

Had Ruth Smith known her? Charlotte wasn't sure how long mermaids lived, but it didn't seem possible.

Excited to tell Ezra, Charlotte hurried along the path toward the cemetery gate. When she was halfway there, she thought she saw something moving in the bushes beside her.

It was a dark shape, so black Charlotte knew it couldn't be a shadow.

The hair on her arms stood on end. It was an eel, a big one. And she was alone.

Trying to stay calm, Charlotte began to walk faster.

The dark shape kept pace with her while slipping from stone to stone, always keeping itself partially hidden.

When the eel was just a few feet away, Charlotte hid behind a granite obelisk, the grave marker of a wealthy sea captain.

Peeking around the stone, she saw that the shadow was moving closer.

To her right, Charlotte noticed another dark shape pressed against the wall of the cemetery chapel, the creature blending into the contours of the small building. To her left, she spotted one more, scarcely visible behind the gray trunk of a giant beech tree. She wondered how many there were, and how long they had been following her.

"Behind you." Charlotte heard a woman's voice. She didn't think anyone else was in the cemetery.

"Hello? Who's there?"

"It's Mistress Ruth. Look behind you."

"Ruth Smith?"

"They're coming. You must turn around."

Sticking straight out of the ground behind Charlotte was a copper pipe with a faucet on the end, meant for watering flowers. A small length of hose was attached to it.

Suddenly understanding what Ruth wanted her to do, Charlotte reached over and turned on the water. She aimed the nozzle at the eel closest to her. Closing her eyes, she squeezed the trigger.

The creature let out a terrible howl. Black smoke rose up from its flesh and a charred, fishy smell permeated the hot summer air. The eel began to melt, its body oozing into the cemetery lawn like the Wicked Witch in *The Wizard of Oz*.

Charlotte let go of the trigger. Looking to her left and then her right, she searched for the other eels, ready to soak them, but they had vanished.

Setting down the hose, Charlotte pressed her head against the cool stone and sat there for a long time.

Chapter 17

The sun was low in the sky when Charlotte climbed the steps to her grandparents' porch. Exhausted and desperate for a shower, she nearly jumped backwards when she saw Charles sitting in Gram's wicker rocking chair. His lip was swollen and purple and he had a nasty bruise on the right side of his jaw.

"Charles? What are you doing here? Did you get in a fight?"

Charles turned toward her, his voice surprisingly calm. "You might want to ask Dad what we're doing here, when he gets back, that is."

Charlotte sat down on the top step. She hadn't seen or talked to her brother since she came to Rocky Harbor.

"If you want to know what happened," said Charles, seeing that Charlotte planned to stay put, "Dad dragged me, Chloe and Diane up here saying it was about time Diane met Gram and Grandpa—since they're getting married—but when we got here all Dad did was try to get Grandpa to give him money. Diane convinced him that he should quit his job at the warehouse and claim disability for that back injury he got a couple of years ago. Grandpa said he'd think about giving Dad the money if he stuck around and helped him out on the boat for the rest of the summer. They got in an argument; Dad got pissed off and knocked Grandpa into the stove. So I let Dad have it. Got in a couple of good right hooks, too."

Charlotte focused on his swollen lip, wondering how hard her father had hit him. "Where's everyone now?"

"Dad and Diane took off after the fight with Grandpa. Gram took Chloe out someplace—I guess she felt bad for her. I think Grandpa's watching TV, but he's OK."

"So what are we going to do?" said Charlotte, worried.

Charles was quiet for a moment and said, "What do you say we go fishing?"

When they had settled into Grandpa's rowboat with their life-jackets on, Charles used one of the wooden oars to push away from the dock.

The air coming up from the cove's surface was cool and briny and felt good inside Charlotte's lungs. Neither Charles nor Charlotte said a word. The only sounds came from the seagulls and the dipping and skimming of the oars.

When they had rowed almost to the middle of the cove, Charles stopped. Though it had only been a month since she'd seen him, he looked older than Charlotte remembered. At sixteen he was already over six feet tall, his dark hair buzzed like a Marine's. Fine hairs darkened his upper lip. He wore long jeans even though the day had been one of the hottest of the summer.

The left sleeve of Charles' T-shirt had gotten bunched up while he was rowing, revealing a farmer's tan and a crescent-shaped brown birthmark. The moon-shaped mark caught Charlotte's eye. She was about to say something about how they both had the same one, but then she noticed he was crying.

"I'm sorry, Charlotte." Charles wiped his eyes with the back of his hand.

Charlotte had seen Charles cry only a handful of times, and not at all since he was about eight years old. She pretended not to notice. "I'm OK, Charles. You don't have to worry about me."

"Who is going to worry about you then? Dad can't even take care of himself. I'm not even sure if our bills are getting paid."

Charlotte put her hand on her brother's shoulder. But before she could think of anything to say, Charles turned in his seat and reached for the fishing rods and tackle box. "It's been a while since we did this, huh?" He stabbed a bloodworm onto Charlotte's hook. "Hell, when I woke up this morning, I never imagined I'd be fishing with my little sister today. This isn't half bad."

"Charles, can I ask you a question?"

"Sure." Charles cast out his line and looked as though he'd finally started to relax, though the bruise on his cheek seemed to be getting darker.

"Do you ever remember hearing anyone talk about a house with golden windows in Rocky Harbor?"

"Golden windows? I don't think so. What's it about?"

"I just heard someone talking about it, that's all. I was wondering if it was a real house or if maybe it's a story or something."

"Got me," said Charles. "But if I hear anything I'll let you know…hey, I've got a bite."

Charles' fishing line had gone taut, the pole bending toward the water in a gentle arc. "Damn. I think it's a big one."

The boat began to drift toward Charles' catch.

"We've moving," said Charlotte. "Maybe we should cut the line."

"Nah," said Charles. "I can handle it. This might be our dinner!"

Charles pulled and reeled, pulled and reeled, and the boat began to travel faster. Whatever was on the end of Charles' line was taking them for a ride.

Trying to hide her growing panic, Charlotte said, "Charles, we really should cut the line. We're going to end up in the open ocean."

"Give me two more minutes. I hate to lose a fish this size." Beads of sweat broke out across Charles' forehead as he struggled, his face turning red.

Suddenly, Charles' line went limp. "Damn. I lost it." He was almost done reeling in the loose line when they heard—and felt—a loud thump on the bottom of the boat.

"What was that?" asked Charlotte, rising from her seat. "Something's under the boat!" Visions of Mortimer's eels, slick and fast in their natural form, raced through her mind.

"Relax," said Charles, grabbing the oars. "It's probably just the big fish I had on my line. I'll row us closer to shore."

He'd only been rowing a minute when they felt another thump on the bottom, hard enough to nearly knock Charlotte's fishing rod over the side.

"I don't think that's a fish," said Charles, peering over the side of the boat. "What the heck could be down there?"

A human hand, pale and cold, emerged from the water and grabbed Charles' forearm. His eyes grew round with panic just before he was pulled over the side into the murky water. Then, with an enormous splash, Charlotte felt something heavy land in the boat.

Eucla sat across from her in the spot where Charles had been.

"What did you do to my brother?" Charlotte asked, wiping seawater off her face. "He could drown."

"Oh, he won't drown," said Eucla. "He's got our blood. As long as he's with my sister he'll be fine."

"Well, tell her to bring him back," said Charlotte. "He doesn't know about you guys. Something like this could land a person in the loony bin."

"He won't remember a thing," said Eucla, shining one of her gold bracelets on the hem of Charlotte's tank top. "When he wakes up he'll just think he fell in the water and that you saved him—as unlikely as that may sound."

"Fine," said Charlotte. "What are you doing here then?"

"Testy today, aren't we?" said Eucla. "I came to get an update on your progress."

Charlotte sighed. "We found the map in the church, just like you said, but when we looked for the bottle in the spot where the map said it would be it wasn't there. All we found was some crazy poem about Mortimer and a house with golden windows. It makes no sense."

"I was afraid of that," said Eucla.

"What? If you knew why didn't you say something?"

"Well, I didn't *know*. I just had a feeling. When you've been around as long as I have you get a sense for these things."

"Great," said Charlotte. "In that case would you happen to have a sense of where the house with the golden windows might be located? That would be helpful."

"Uh, not really. I don't visit very many houses—as you can imagine. But you should really get on it. Those eels are getting to be a real nuisance. I've had to kill eight of them just today."

Before Charlotte could say another word, Eucla launched herself over the side and was gone. A second later, Charles appeared in the water next to the rowboat. The bruises on his face and lip had completely disappeared.

Charlotte helped him into the boat. "Are you OK, Charles? You fell overboard."

"The last thing I remember I had that big fish on the line. Did I lose it?"

"You did. But you put up a good fight."

A look of recognition came over Charles' face. "Right. I'll tell you one thing, this salt water is great. My lip feels like new."

Chapter 18

Charlotte sat on the bench outside Costa's Market waiting for Ezra to get out of work. On the phone the night before he said he had something important to tell her. The store was busy and the few street parking spots near the front entrance were always occupied—as soon as one person pulled out, another pulled in. A woman driving a navy BMW pulled into the spot in front of Charlotte just as Ezra came out of the store with Edward Kitchen.

"Hi, Charlotte," said Edward. He had a ketchup stain on the pocket of his work shirt. Charlotte hadn't seen him since the first day she'd gone into Costa's with her grandmother. He didn't seem to have improved much over the past month.

"Hi," she said. "What's going on, Ezra?"

Ezra sat down next to Charlotte on the bench, leaving Edward standing. "I was talking to Ed at work the other day and I happened to mention we were looking for a house with golden windows."

Charlotte shot him a look. She hoped Ezra was smart enough to know better than to tell Edward what they had been up to.

"I told him it was for your summer history project—for school," Ezra continued.

"That's right," said Edward. "He told me all about it. I had no idea you were such a history buff, Charlotte. If I'd known I would have suggested a few books. I have a nice collection at home."

"Ed was telling me that he's been working on a project at the town library," said Ezra. "He's helping them put their archives online. He thinks there's something there that might help you."

"I'm helping Mrs. Hunt, the librarian, set up a Rocky Harbor history website," said Edward proudly. "It's going to have everything: old photos, property deeds, news clippings, maps, stories. It will all be searchable by subject, keyword and date. Right now it's just on the library's server, but we're going to make it live in a few weeks. I'll call Mrs. Hunt and ask her if you can look at it. I'm sure she won't mind. I'll tell her we're old friends."

"I had no idea you were so good with computers," said Charlotte. She had always assumed that Edward would end up like most kids in town, working on a lobster boat by the time he was sixteen.

"I had to do something to pass the time all those days when my dad was at sea," Edward said. "Learning to write code was as good as anything."

Charlotte leafed through a copy of *The Great Gatsby* that someone had left at the circulation desk while one of the clerks at the library went to get Mrs. Hunt.

The librarian was a tall, slender woman in her late forties. Her straight hair, peppered with gray, fell into her eyes whenever she leaned over. She smelled faintly of lemons and wore a white blouse and a green pencil skirt that came just past her knees.

"Doing a project for school?" Mrs. Hunt brushed the hair from her eyes and entered her password into the computer.

"For extra credit," said Charlotte. "Edward Kitchen wanted me to tell you that he says hello."

At the mention of Edward's name Mrs. Hunt smiled. "Edward has helped us so much with this project. Take as much time as you want. Don't hesitate to call me if you need anything."

On the website's homepage was an old black-and-white photo of Rocky Harbor's downtown. No gold windows. But she did spot Costa's Market in the foreground. It had a different sign, but the building was the same. Nathan Jacobs' Seafood Market was there, too, the large wooden sign in front bearing the likeness of a giant mermaid holding a fish. Charlotte would have to remember to ask Mr. Jacobs what had happened to it.

In the search bar at the top of the page Charlotte typed "golden windows" and hit enter.

A number of results came up. One was a *Gloucester Times* article from the 1980s about a ship carrying Spanish gold coins that had run aground by Light Island. No one had ever found it.

There were stories about pirates hiding gold treasure in the hidden sea caves that dotted Rocky Harbor's shoreline, and photos of gold bracelets, chains and coins that had supposedly been pulled up in lobster traps.

Charlotte went to reach for her water bottle and noticed it had fallen onto the floor.

That's weird, she thought, picking it up before trying another search, this time typing "house with golden windows."

Only one result came up.

On the screen was a scan of a hand-written letter dated September 19, 1799. Charlotte had to squint to read the ornate cursive:

Mr. William Gregory Smith
919 Charles Street
Beacon Hill
Boston, Massachusetts

My Dearest Nephew,
I know you are a married man now and have a number of responsibilities relating to your growing mercantile business, so I will do my best to keep this brief. Since I have gotten older, and am no longer able to work long days tending to the sick, I seem to lose track of the passing time.

I write to you about a matter most urgent. Because you are my sister's son, and with her passing are now my closest living relative, I see fit to trust you with this burden I have carried nearly all of my days—since a time when I had the strength to bear such a heavy load on my own.

I speak, of course, about the blue bottle and the map that discloses its location. I know that your mother told you their story many times in your youth. Then, I imagine it must have seemed like a fairy tale. But it is real, my dear William, as real as the salt in the sea.

Now that I will soon be in the company of our Lord, I must entrust this knowledge to one whom I would trust with my own life.

I must also warn you. During the writing of this letter I was visited by a premonition most dark. While harvesting wild sumac by the shore, a raven came and perched by my side. It has been said that the birds are agents of the Devil, but this one was a messenger.

As I gathered the shorn branches and prepared to return home, the dark bird began to gyrate, like a demon possessed. From its beak came a fountain of blood.

Its essence spilled out upon the stones, the raven prepared to pass on. And as it crossed over into another world—to meet the Lord or to a much darker place I cannot say—the blood that it had spilled came to life in the form of a red serpent.

As the serpent took on strength, it slithered along the ground in a most alarming way until it had reached the very edge of my slippers. And then, my dearest Nephew, that serpent did indeed speak.

"Mortimer is near," it said.

In my fright, I hurried back to my cottage by the cove, praying the incident had been nothing more than the imaginings of an old woman. But in my heart I knew it had been real.

I made haste to retrieve the bottle from where it had been hidden by Boyd Morgan in a crook of the old elm, and entrusted Mr. Morgan's map to the Reverend Brown for safekeeping in the church. I have taken it upon myself to place the bottle most carefully in the root cellar of the house with the golden windows that lies at the tip of the Annisquam.

You are the only person, dear William, whom I will trust with this most serious confession. Keep this letter close to your heart always.

Your Loving Aunt,
Ruth

Charlotte rubbed her eyes. Why hadn't anyone recognized the letter? Edward and Mrs. Hunt had probably just found it in a box someplace and scanned it without even reading it.

As she waited for the letter to appear in the printer tray, Charlotte shut down the Rocky Harbor history site, worried that someone may have been reading over her shoulder. She folded the printout and put it in her pocket.

Charlotte stepped out of the air-conditioned library into the midday sun. From the top of the building's granite steps she could see the harbor. Yachts and lobster boats were scattered along its surface like toys in a duck pond. In the distance she heard a muted humming sound, like the whirring blades of a helicopter.

Charlotte looked up to find a long-legged boy running toward her down the sidewalk. It was Ezra. What was he doing running in this heat?

"Charlotte!" he said, gasping for breath.

"What's going on?" Charlotte put her hand on his shoulder as he doubled over, trying to breathe.

"It's your grandfather—the lobster boat's missing."

Charlotte wasn't sure she'd heard him right. "Missing? What are you talking about?"

"While you were in the library there was another tremor. It churned up some pretty big waves. A few boats—went under."

"You must be wrong, Ezra. I didn't feel any tremor. I'm sure I would have noticed something like that."

"You were in the library basement – with no windows," said Ezra, standing up straight. "You probably couldn't tell."

Charlotte froze, remembering how her water bottle had fallen to the floor.

"Come back to the store with me. Mr. Costa will drive you home. You need to wait with your grandmother for the Coast Guard to call."

She took Ezra's hand and followed him to Costa's. She didn't notice that her neatly folded copy of Ruth Smith's letter had slipped onto the sidewalk.

Chapter 19

Morton Bathyal sat in front on an oscillating fan in his office trying to keep cool. The air conditioning system at the antiques store was almost as old as the building. Elaborate seascapes that Bathyal had collected over the years decorated his office walls. On his desk was the sea captain's diary that had led him to Rocky Harbor with its account of the *Gertrude Chance* wreck.

The increasing number of earthquakes shaking up Rocky Harbor concerned him. He wasn't troubled by the effects they would have on the town's people. Their pointless, ridiculous lives didn't interest him. What was important was the effect they could have on the bottle. If it was hidden inside a building, and that building collapsed, there was a good chance it would be destroyed.

The brass bells attached to the front door jingled. Bathyal rose from his seat to greet the customer and instead saw Anguilla entering the shop. He had a folded piece of paper in his right hand.

With great flourish, Anguilla set the paper on the counter by the cash register.

"What do we have here?" asked Bathyal.

"The girl dropped this," said Anguilla. "One of my—associates—picked it up."

Anguilla looked terrible. The heat wasn't doing him any favors, Bathyal thought. It was a wonder that someone hadn't reported him—or any of the other eels they'd sent out—to the police.

Bathyal picked up the paper. A thin-lipped smile spread across his face as he realized what he had before him.

"Excellent work, Anguilla. They've done most of the hard work for us—just as I'd hoped. All we need to do is find the location of this house before she and the boy do. All of our dreams are about to come true, Anguilla. I can feel it."

Bathyal sat down on the padded stool behind the counter. The heat and excitement had made him lightheaded.

"We have another advantage," said Anguilla, mopping seawater from his brow with a paper napkin. "The girl's grandfather—his boat went missing during the last quake. She's going to be busy for a while—too busy to search for an old house."

Bathyal cracked a wide smile. "Soon, Anguilla, you and I will be the rulers of our own world."

Chapter 20

The ride home in the back of Mr. Costa's Cadillac was a blur. Charlotte knew Ezra was next to her, and recognized that Mr. Costa was talking, but she had no idea what he was saying. When they pulled up to the green Victorian at 29 Wharf Street she got out of the car and wandered into the house without making a sound. A Coast Guard patrol car was parked in the driveway. Her grandmother was on the couch in the living room. Two Coast Guard officers sat at the kitchen table drinking lemonade. Gram had drawn the shades to keep the heat out. The house was dark, like stepping into a cave.

Charlotte stood in the middle of the living room, feeling numb. The television was tuned to the local cable news channel. The marine radio droned in the corner.

When she saw Charlotte, Gram got up and put her arms around her but said nothing. Finally she said to Ezra, "Why don't you go to the kitchen and get something to drink."

Gram led Charlotte to the rocking chair. "I called your father. He's coming with Charles."

Charlotte nodded. "I'm going outside for a minute. I need some air."

If it wasn't bad enough that her grandfather was missing, now she was going to have to deal with Diane and Chloe, too. Charlotte hoped they would stay home.

Out on the dock, Charlotte took the gold mirror out of her backpack. The glass was cloudy and cold. She held the handle firmly in her right hand and said, "Eucla, please come. I need you."

Charlotte heard the screen door to the porch swing closed and saw Ezra coming across the lawn. He sat down beside her.

Just when Charlotte was sure Eucla wasn't going to come, the water beside the dock erupted into a mass of bubbles. Eucla's head popped out of the murky water, followed by her arms. Her porcelain hands gripped the side of the dock, and she hauled herself up, nearly knocking Charlotte and Ezra into the cove with her tail.

"Oh, you've got a friend," said Eucla, motioning toward Ezra with her head. "He's a cute one. I wish you'd warned me. I'm not looking my best today."

Ezra was astonished. Even though Charlotte had told him about Eucla—and he had believed her—he hadn't been prepared to actually meet a real, live mermaid. Eucla's fingers glittered with glistening jeweled rings. A live herring that had been caught in her hair struggled to free itself, flapping and twisting its silver body. She reached up, grabbed the fish and bit off its head.

After she swallowed, Eucla said, "So what's happening? All this rumbling is starting to get pretty annoying."

"I need you to help me." Charlotte fought to keep from crying.

Eucla stuffed the headless herring into the pouch strapped to her waist. "What's wrong?" The mermaid's forehead crinkled up in a way that made Charlotte wonder if she really was old enough to have known Ruth Smith.

"My grandpa's boat," Charlotte began. "The waves from the earthquake . . ."

Eucla held her hand up, indicating that she'd heard enough. She took the pouch from around her waist and dumped its contents out on the dock. The decapitated herring came flying out, followed by ten silver bottle caps, a pile of mismatched glass beads and a Canadian quarter. A gold hoop earring glistened in a puddle of seawater.

She shook the pouch a second time and out came a few shiny bits of an aluminum can and the head of a Barbie doll. "Would you look at how shiny this is," Eucla said, holding a square of aluminum foil up to the light.

Still not seeing what she was looking for, the mermaid reached into the pouch and pulled out a small mirror, much like the gold one still in Charlotte's hand.

As Eucla held the mirror, its glass began to glow. She spoke in muted tones. The words she used were ancient. To Charlotte, they sounded like the low hush of the sea, and waves crashing on the rocks.

Eucla looked up at Charlotte and said, "He's alive. He's hanging onto a life ring someplace off the coast. The water's choppy—too cold. I don't know how much longer he'll be able to hold on. There's no sign of the boat."

Eucla began shoving the items back into her pouch at furious pace. At the last second, she decided to throw the decapitated herring into the water.

"Do you want this?" Eucla held the Barbie doll's head out to Ezra. "I need to make some room."

"Uh, thanks."

When Eucla had all of her things put away she hauled herself over the side of the dock, soaking Charlotte and Ezra.

"Sorry," Eucla said when her head bobbed above the surface and she saw how wet they were. "Don't worry. We'll get him."

When Charlotte and Ezra walked back up to the house Charlotte's father's car was in the driveway.

"My dad's here," said Charlotte. "You might want to go home."

"OK. I understand. You want to be alone with your family."

"No, that's not it. He's just been acting like kind of a jerk lately."

The truth was that Charlotte was embarrassed to have Ezra meet her father, especially if Diane and Chloe were with him.

As Ezra turned to walk down the driveway, Charles burst out the porch door.

"Charlotte! The Coast Guard has him! He's on the rocks by White Island. They have no idea how he got there."

Chapter 21

"Thanks for coming with me," said Charlotte. She and Ezra sat in the waiting area on the fourth floor of Cape Ann Hospital. Gram had sent them to keep Grandpa company while she went out and did some errands. Ezra plopped his backpack between his feet.

"You can go in now." A plump nurse with a pleasant face appeared in the hallway. "Your grandfather is very tired so don't expect too much. It's going to be a few days before he's feeling like himself again."

"I'll wait here," said Ezra. "They have the new copy of, uh, Better Homes & Gardens." He pointed to the magazines fanned out on the table. "I've been wondering what to do with my hydrangeas."

Charlotte stepped around the privacy curtain. Grandpa was sitting up in bed, his left arm encased in a fiberglass cast. The TV remote rested on the sheets near his right hand. Along his left cheek stretched an angry, red slash held together with Steri-Strips. He noticed Charlotte staring at the wound.

"Aw, don't worry about that," said Grandpa, smiling, pointing to his cheek. "Doctor says it will heal up nice. Even if it doesn't, the scar'll make me look like a tough guy."

Charlotte leaned across the bed and gave him a hug. Seeing him in bed all broken and bruised made her realize how close she had come to losing him.

Charlotte's lower lip curled.

"Shhh. Everything's going to be OK," said Grandpa. "The insurance will pay for a new boat—though your father has been trying to convince me to just take the money and retire. I don't want to do that, but with my arm like this I'm starting to think he's got a point. Without help I don't see how I'm going to be able to fish again any time soon." Grandpa winced as he tried to adjust his position.

"I'm not upset about the boat," said Charlotte, twirling a loose thread from Grandpa's blanket around her index finger. "Grandpa, what happened? I didn't think I'd see you ever again."

"To be honest, Charlotte I'm not sure. One minute everything was fine. Next thing you know, a wall of water knocked the boat over like it was one of those remote control toys. I managed to pull the life ring off the stern rail before it went under. It gets murky after that—except I have this strange memory of a pair of hands pulling me to the surface. I saw two girls swimming. They were speaking a language I didn't know, but I felt like I could understand them. But now I have no idea what they said. I must have hit my head pretty hard."

Grandpa picked up from the bedside table a smooth granite pebble strung on a piece of twine. "When I woke up this was around my neck."

Charlotte turned the bead over in her hands. She recognized it as one that Eucla had been wearing. "You should wear it, Grandpa. I think it's good luck."

Chapter 22

Other than his arm still being in the cast, Grandpa was feeling like his old self again within a week. Without his lobster boat, and unable to do much else, he sat in the living room reading most of the day; a stack of *Reader's Digest* magazines sat on the table beside his recliner. Gram asked Edward Kitchen to come over and help with a few jobs around the yard, even though Charlotte insisted she could take care of them herself.

The smell of gasoline and freshly cut grass drifted up to the porch. Charlotte sat watching Edward push Grandpa's lawnmower back and forth across the yard.

Somehow she'd misplaced the copy of Ruth Smith's letter she'd printed at the library. She wanted to ask Edward if he thought Mrs. Hunt would let her go back and print another one, but she didn't want to be pushy. At least she remembered what the letter said: The house with the golden windows had been someplace on the Annisquam Peninsula.

"Gram, I'm going for a walk," Charlotte hollered through the open kitchen window. "I'll be back before supper."

Charlotte's plan was to search the length of the cove for signs of an old house: depressions in the ground, rotten planks, piles of old foundation stones. Although the old fish cannery was located there, she wasn't exactly sure where Annisquam began, and she didn't want to miss anything. She was going to keep at it until she'd searched every inch of ground.

Charlotte climbed up and over the granite boulders lining the shore, past the old white church. She took extra care to examine the few houses that stood on the bluff, but didn't think any of them looked old enough to have been mentioned in Ruth's letter.

When she got to the boarded up Annisquam Fish Cannery, Charlotte decided she was going to have to turn around. The rundown seafood processing plant was located right at the spot where the cove met the open ocean. There was no more ground to cover.

Charlotte switched her backpack strap to her opposite shoulder and decided to walk along the rocks closest to the water, which tended to be smaller and easier to navigate. Looking up at the rotting cannery, she saw the tops of maple trees growing up through the holes in the corrugated metal roof. Huge sections of the exterior walls had collapsed. Through the openings, Charlotte could make out the silhouette of the old assembly line. Wheeled bins once used to transport thousands of pounds of fish littered the factory floor like stalled bumper cars. Years of salt air had rusted them to their tracks.

As she was about to head home, Charlotte noticed something else. The windows on the cannery's top floor, the ones that still had glass in them, were glowing orange.

In the hour or so that she'd been walking, the sun had dropped closer to the horizon. And at that moment, it was at the perfect angle to reflect off the windows.

Maybe there had been a house on this spot before the cannery had been built? Maybe a few houses. The land was level and would have been easy to build on.

Charlotte had to find a way to get inside.

She walked around the perimeter of the building looking for a way through the chain link fence, ignoring the red-lettered "No Trespassing" signs.

When she had walked a full circle with no luck, she decided to climb the fence. It was topped with barbed wire, but she was sure she could handle it.

Tossing her backpack over the top, Charlotte grabbed the fence and began hoisting herself up, hand over foot, until she reached the top. That was the easy part.

She eased one leg at a time over the rusty barbs at the top, hoping no one would see her. The metal links dug into the soft flesh of her hands, but she had no choice but to hang on.

Once she was safely on the ground she picked up her backpack and went to take a look around. At first glance, Charlotte could almost have believed the factory had just closed for the night, the workers set to return in the morning. The assembly line looked almost as if it could have started rolling on its own.

But as she made her way around the building she realized much of the factory's equipment was gone: stolen, or hauled away and sold for scrap. Bits of blue sky showed through the patchwork of holes in the ceiling, creating patterns of light and dark inside the building that made it difficult to see more than twenty feet ahead.

Charlotte came across an office, the desk and chair still in place. On the wall, just inside the door, was an old punch clock once used by employees to record their daily shifts.

Though it had been a hot day, the office was cool and damp. The cushion on the chair gave off a putrid, musty smell. The green floor tiles were marred by bird droppings and brown water stains. Against one wall was a steel bookcase. A framed photograph, coated in dust, was propped up on one of the shelves.

Taking the photo down, Charlotte wiped away the thick layer of filth with the hem of her T-shirt. It was a black-and-white picture of a small house. Made entirely of stones, the cottage was two stories tall with a small porch on the front. A flower garden grew beside it. Charlotte could see the ocean in the background, beyond the sparse trees at the rear of the property.

Flipping the picture over, Charlotte found something written on the back in pencil. It was too dark in the office to see what it was. She brought it out to the factory floor and stood beneath one of the ceiling holes.

Even in the sunlight, the inscription was hard to read. After a minute she was able to make out:

Peterson summer house at Annisquam, 1860.

She unzipped her backpack and slipped the picture inside.

It was getting late and she'd told Gram she'd be back in time for supper.

Not wanting to throw her backpack over the fence again for fear of breaking the glass in the photo frame, Charlotte slipped both arms through the straps and secured the pack snugly to her back. Climbing the fence was easier than it had been the first time. But when she got to the top something made her freeze in her tracks.

The breeze coming off the cove had picked up, bringing with it a sharp, fishy odor. Charlotte teetered on top of the fence, one leg on either side, knowing the smell could only mean one thing.

The problem for Charlotte was she didn't know which side of the fence the eel was on. If she continued climbing down the cove side, and the eel was there waiting for her, she'd have no place to hide. If it was on the cannery side and she decided to climb back down the way she came, she'd be trapped inside the fence with the monster.

Minutes passed, and the smell grew stronger. Charlotte began to worry not just about the eel but that someone would see her on top of the fence and call the police. The shadows were growing longer. Her grandmother would be wondering where she was.

Deciding to take her chances on the cove side, Charlotte swung her leg over the top and caught her shin on the barbed wire, tearing a deep gash just below her knee. Pain ripped through her leg, but she stopped herself from crying out, afraid of drawing the attention of the people on sailboats in the cove. She clenched her teeth and continued climbing down.

Stepping carefully onto the rocks, Charlotte tested her footing to make sure she didn't step on anything loose or slippery. The fishy smell was getting stronger. The eel had to be close by. If she could make it to the white church, she could climb up onto the bluff and take the road home. She only needed to make it that far.

The first few yards along the rocks weren't bad. There was still enough light for Charlotte to see where she was going and she made good time. But as she struggled to climb a particularly tall ledge, her leg throbbing, she felt something cold and wet wrap itself around her ankle.

The eel's grip was like iron. Remembering the cemetery, she tried to think of a way to get her water bottle out of her backpack without letting go of the rock.

Charlotte pulled her leg up, trying to break the eel's grip. But the harder she pulled, the tighter the creature's grasp seemed to be. Its smell was overpowering, forcing Charlotte to take tiny sips of air through her mouth.

Charlotte's fingernails scraped along the rocks as the eel pulled her down.

The night was closing in.

Chapter 23

Trapped in a crevice among the boulders lining the cove, Charlotte looked the eel in the face—or what seemed to be its face. In the failing light the beast seemed to be little more than a dark shadow with glowing yellow eyes.

"What do you want?" Charlotte finally asked. She began to slip the strap of her backpack off of her left shoulder, hoping the eel wouldn't notice.

A horrible gurgling sound erupted from the eel's throat, making Charlotte jump. "We wait," it said. At least that's what Charlotte thought she heard behind the sputtering in its gullet.

For what? Charlotte thought, not wanting to ask any other questions. She didn't want to know.

The strap of her backpack nearly all the way off, she was going to have to think of an escape plan. Once she squirted the eel with the water bottle there was no telling what it would do. She would need to get away fast, up and over the rocks and out of its range before it was able to follow her.

She only had enough water in the bottle to take care of the eel in front of her. She prayed that there weren't any others.

Charlotte slid her backpack the rest of the way off and placed it gently in front of her, trying not to make any sudden movements.

A low, watery sound erupted from someplace inside the eel as Charlotte slowly undid the zipper on her bag. She reached inside with her right hand, glad it was almost dark, and grasped her plastic sport bottle.

Slipping one of the backpack's straps back over her right shoulder, she flicked the bottle's cap up with her thumb.

Holding the bottle, Charlotte sat very still. She aimed the nozzle at the eel's yellow eyes, and squeezed.

When the fresh water hit it, the monster let out a terrible howl. Smoke, smelling like burnt seaweed, rose up from its flesh. It let go of Charlotte's ankle.

Charlotte scrambled up and over the large rock she'd had so much trouble climbing before. Fearful that she was being followed, she ran and jumped over boulders like a mountain goat, her backpack bouncing behind her.

The eel's stench faded as she approached the bluff where the white church overlooked the cove. She scrambled up the rocks, grabbing clumps of long grass and scraggly roots for support.

The road leading from St. Peter's to the downtown was quiet and empty. Mosquitoes buzzed around Charlotte's face and ears. She was dirty and hungry, her feet crunching the bits of gravel and broken quahog shells that covered the road.

As soon as Charlotte came through the porch door she heard her grandmother's voice.

"Is that you, Charlotte?"

"Yeah, Gram!" Charlotte hoped she wouldn't say anything else. All she wanted was to go upstairs and take care of the cut on her leg without Gram seeing it.

When Charlotte had made it to the middle of the stairway Gram said, "Come down for dinner in fifteen minutes!"

So much for a long, hot shower, Charlotte thought as she pulled the framed photograph from her bag. She sighed with relief when she saw that the glass hadn't been broken.

Maybe one of her grandparents would know where the house was.

To cover her bandaged leg and the scrapes on her arms, Charlotte put on jeans and a long sleeve flannel shirt before she went downstairs.

"I know you're getting older now, Charlotte. But I wish you'd call next time you're going to be a bit late," said Gram. "With everything you see on the news it's hard not to worry."

Her hands buried in thick oven mitts, Gram pulled a casserole dish of baked beans from the oven and placed it in the center of the table. The sweet, smoky aroma of bacon and cooked sugar filled the small kitchen.

"Would you mind asking your grandfather to get a jar of pickles from the cellar?"

Charlotte's grandfather was watching the news with Melville the cat curled up beside him.

"Hi, Grandpa," said Charlotte.

Her grandfather held his index finger to his lips. He lowered his voice. "Don't tell Gram he's on the couch," he said, pointing to the cat.

Charlotte smiled and nodded. "Gram wants you to go downstairs and get some pickles." Handing him the photograph, she said, "Do you know anything about this house? I think it used to be near the cannery."

Grandpa reached for his glasses and put them on. "Makes me think back to when Gram worked at the Annisquam cannery. This house used to belong to the family that owned the place. Was their summer home. The house is still there behind the cannery building—overgrown with trees in the woods."

Chapter 24

"Tell Ezra he's welcome to join us for dinner later," said Gram as she pulled the red Buick up to the curb in front of Mrs. Bouchard's house. She was on her way to the eye doctor in Gloucester and had offered to drop Charlotte off on the way.

"Hi there!" Ezra came to the door wearing loose khaki shorts and a white polo shirt that accentuated his tan. He smelled like soap. "Let's sit on the porch. My grandmother's in the living room doing story hour with the kids from the daycare center. Sometimes they walk over here from Water Street. We'd have to be really quiet if we sat in the house."

Charlotte sat down on the wicker sofa facing the cove, her back sinking into the soft cushion.

"What happened to you?" Ezra asked, pointing to the bandage on her shin and the cuts on her hands and arms. "It looks like you've been digging ditches with your bare hands."

Charlotte pulled her backpack onto her lap and took out the photo from the cannery. When she was done explaining what happened the day before, Ezra's expression grew serious.

"You could have gotten killed. What if you didn't have that water with you? Tell you what, you and I are going back there tomorrow and we're going to find that bottle."

Before she left home the next day Charlotte filled her backpack with as many bottles of water as she could carry, the weight causing the bag to hang low between her shoulders. By the time she and Ezra made it to the rocks beside Barnacle Bob's she was covered in sweat, her powder blue T-shirt turned dark. From that point, they still had at least twenty minutes of climbing to do.

Ezra was soon walking far ahead of Charlotte. To keep cool, Charlotte pulled her dark hair back into a ponytail, but her neck was still sweating. Hot droplets rolled down her sides and into the waistband of her shorts.

"Are you coming?" Ezra hollered from up ahead. He was waiting for her to catch up.

When Charlotte got to where he was standing she was winded. "Sorry," she said. "This bag is really heavy."

Ezra lifted her pack from her shoulders. "That must weigh thirty pounds. You need to get rid of some of those. If anything comes after us you won't be able to get away." He unzipped Charlotte's pack and took out four one-liter bottles, leaving two inside. "We can pick them up on the way back." He nestled the bottles into a crevice between two rocks.

When Charlotte had safely reached the ground on the cannery side of the fence, Ezra said, "I didn't know you could climb a fence like that. I thought I was going to have to help you."

Charlotte crossed her arms. "I can do a lot of things, you know."

"I didn't mean it that way," said Ezra, landing on both feet beside Charlotte. "It's just that most girls I know—they wouldn't even get halfway up."

The area surrounding the cannery was eerily quiet. Only the distant sound of the surf and the occasional cackling of a gull broke the silence. Neither Charlotte nor Ezra spoke as they wandered through the building looking for a door that led to the land behind it.

When they reached the office where Charlotte had found the photograph, Charlotte said, "Maybe there's a map of the cannery in here someplace. We need to figure out how to get onto the grounds and over to that house."

Sunlight streaming through a hole on the far side of the building created eerie shadows on the office wall. Goosebumps erupted along Ezra's forearms and thighs.

Ezra nodded. He didn't want to let on how nervous he was. He'd been in a lot of old buildings, even falling-down dumpy ones like this, but there was something about the Annisquam Fish

Cannery that made the hairs on the back of his neck stand straight up.

They walked down one hollow corridor after another, finding nothing but rotting planks and musty hills of bat guano. Eventually they came across a painted steel door.

Charlotte tried the handle. "It's not locked." She turned the knob slowly, not knowing what would greet her on the other side. Ezra squeezed his eyes shut.

It was a janitor's closet, full of petrified string mops and cleaning solutions that had turned brown in their bottles. "Let's keep looking," Ezra said.

They crossed the packaging floor to the other side of the building. Metal stems from the light fixtures that once hung from the ceiling were scattered sporadically along the roof beams, like uneven spokes on a wheel

Charlotte spotted the stairs first. At the far end of the packaging room was a wide set of steps leading downward, oak handrails along each side. Even with the natural light coming in from the ceiling and walls, not much was visible beyond the third or fourth step.

"We're going to need your flashlight," said Charlotte to Ezra as she walked toward the stairs.

"Are you sure you want to go down there?" Ezra unzipped his backpack and pulled out the flashlight. "What if the batteries die or something?"

Charlotte turned and looked at him. "I'm sure it will be fine," she said.

She was trying to be brave. Something in the cannery had changed since the day before. The air felt heavy, like a weight pushing on them from all directions.

She approached the steps carefully, grasping the handrail as she descended. Ezra stayed close behind her.

The top few stairs were dry, but as Charlotte and Ezra stepped toward the darkness they became damp and slippery, the concrete walls covered in patches of black slime. The air was cold and wet, like a fog-covered beach. Within the glowing circle of Ezra's flashlight, centipedes and silverfish skittered across the stairwell. By the twelfth step, the walls' slime coat had spread to the stairs. Ezra and Charlotte stepped down from the final step into the cannery's basement, the sound of running water all around them. "It's seawater," said Ezra. "Look at the walls."

Streams of water poured through cracks in the walls and floor. Clumps of white barnacles grew along the lower part of the walls, along with clusters of mussels, their shells white from living in the darkness. Tiny crabs, colorless as ghosts, scurried through puddles with their sideways walks.

"From the looks of this place it fills up with water when the tide comes in," said Ezra. "And," he looked down at his watch, "it looks like the tide's started to do just that." The water rushing through a fist-sized crevice in the wall beside them had begun to flow faster. In the few minutes they stood there, the depth of the seawater on the floor increased by an inch.

Charlotte took a deep breath. "Let's just take a quick look around and see what we can find. We can come back tomorrow if we have to."

They sloshed down the dark hallway, cold seawater seeping into their sneakers. Attached to the walls near the floor were pale sea stars, their spindly legs reaching out into the darkness.

They came to a double set of wooden doors covered in barnacles and the same black slime that coated the rest of the basement. Charlotte wriggled the doors back and forth. Sunlight appeared in the inch-wide opening between them.

"Look!" she said to Ezra. "This leads outside. We have to find a way to get it open."

Ezra said, "I think there's a bolt cutter in the carriage house at my grandmother's house—at my grandfather's old workbench."

"That will take forever. We'll have to wait until tomorrow."

Reluctantly Charlotte turned around, following Ezra back the way they'd come.

The water was nearly up to the middle of Charlotte's shins, making walking hard and slow. Ezra's long legs made it easier for him, but he was still much slower than he'd been on the way in.

From the top step, they watched as seawater filled the basement hallway and covered the lower steps.

"We almost didn't make it out," said Ezra. He set his backpack down and slid down to sit beside it, his legs sprawling out in front of him.

Charlotte sat beside him, drawing her legs to her chest. She stretched her hand out and placed it on Ezra's knee, resting her head on his shoulder.

Chapter 25

Charlotte woke with a start. Her damp clothes had drawn the heat away from her body while she'd slept and she shivered with cold. The sun was low in the sky, making her think it must be late afternoon.

Ezra's backpack was still on the floor beside her, but he was gone.

"Ezra!" Charlotte's voice echoed through the deserted factory, making the abandoned building seem lonelier than it already was. When there was no reply, she picked up Ezra's backpack and set out to find him.

Gram was going to be worried about her if she didn't get home soon. She wondered how long it would take for someone to find her if something awful were to happen.

Charlotte made her way across the old production floor, calling, "Ezra! Where are you?"

Ezra wouldn't have gone home without her. Maybe he'd gone exploring and twisted his ankle.

She thought about climbing the fence and going back to her grandparents' house, hoping Ezra would figure it out and eventually follow her. But Charlotte knew there might be eels everywhere, hiding among the rocks, waiting for her.

Charlotte shined the flashlight down the staircase that led to the basement. The tide had receded a bit. She left the backpacks at the top of the stairs, took the flashlight and began to climb down.

The water was still up past her ankles, but rather than the sound of rushing water she'd heard before, everything was quiet when Charlotte got to the moldering oak doors.

Peering through the crack between them, Charlotte saw a set of stairs leading upward. Hay-colored grass grew up through the spaces between the steps.

She pressed her shoulder against the center point of the doors, hoping to widen the crack and get a better look.

As she pushed, she heard a creaking sound, like a nail coming loose from a plank. The corroded iron hinge that attached the door on the right to its casing had started to pull free.

Walking to the far side of the dank hallway, Charlotte got a running start. She slammed her hip and shoulder against the door as hard as she could.

"Ouch!" She rubbed her arm. The door was more solid than it looked. But she'd managed to move the hinge nearly another inch.

After a few more painful slams, Charlotte was exhausted, the hinge only having moved slightly away from the wall, certainly not enough for her to be able to pry open the door.

As she stood trying to catch her breath she heard footsteps upstairs.

Charlotte prayed that it was Ezra.

Careful not to splash, Charlotte crept toward the staircase, her fingers pressed against the slippery wall for balance. When she came to a point where she could see the light shining down from above, the footsteps grew louder. She stood with her back to the wall, trying to blend into the shadows.

Into her line of vision stepped Morton Bathyal, his wire-rim glasses high on the bridge of his nose. Charlotte, afraid even to breathe, stretched her neck out in hope of seeing who might be with him. But she didn't have to.

"Mr. Bouchard," said Bathyal, his thick English accent heavy with sarcasm, "you mean to tell me that you have no idea why you're in the cannery building? Surely, you and Miss Hale came in here looking for something. I'm inclined to think that if you and your girlfriend were merely looking for a romantic hideaway you could find a more suitable one than this. Am I right?"

Bathyal had Ezra! Charlotte swallowed hard. Her thoughts whirled like a stormy sea as she considered her options. If Bathyal was up there, his creepy assistant, Anguilla, and the other eels were sure to be, too. Ezra didn't know where she was, so he couldn't give her away, but it wouldn't be very long until they figured it out, anyway. Her only hope was to find a way to get through those doors.

It was then that she heard the first awful sounds: the clanking and crashing of metal; glass breaking—noises that could only mean another earthquake. She closed her eyes and prayed the basement walls were strong enough to hold up.

As the earth shook, the voices upstairs grew louder, but Charlotte couldn't make out what they were saying. There was a horrific crash, as if part of the building's corrugated steel ceiling had come down, followed by terrible wailing. Someone had been badly hurt.

Using the chaos as cover, Charlotte retreated back into the underground passageway, moving quickly through the ankle-deep water. Not daring to turn on the flashlight, she depended on the dim light shining down from the top of the stairway to see. But as she approached the double set of oak doors she saw that the late afternoon sunlight was streaming into the hallway.

The quake had finished what she'd started. The door on the right was free of its hinges. The door slab, still completely intact, lay atop the granite brick stairs leading to the land behind the cannery.

Charlotte stepped over the fallen door, the mustiness of the cellar giving way to the fresh scent of salt spray and warm grass. When she reached the top of the steps, she was greeted by a beautiful view of the cove at the spot where it met the ocean. Gulls soared overhead on currents warm of air. Along the horizon, Charlotte could see the tiny colored specks of sailboats.

A few hundred feet in front of Charlotte was a patch of woods. Not the dense type of old forest that still grows up in Canada and Maine, but the new growth kind common in southern

New England, where the land had once been cleared. Someplace among the maples and birches was the old stone house, or what was left of it.

The sun warmed Charlotte's face as she tried to decide what to do. She didn't have her backpack, or anything else besides Ezra's flashlight. And she couldn't go back inside.

Another loud crash rocked the cannery as an additional section of ceiling came crashing down. She heard voices coming from the basement hallway. Someone had discovered the underground passageway. Soon they would be right behind her.

No longer thinking of Mortimer or Ezra or that it would be getting dark soon, Charlotte ran toward the cover of the trees.

Chapter 26

It was much cooler among the trees than in the grassy field. The scent of decaying leaves and damp soil filled Charlotte's lungs as she fought her way through the underbrush. There was no path to walk on. She used her arms to hold back the slim lower branches of maple saplings, wondering what the place looked like before the trees had grown.

The sound of the surf on the ocean side of the peninsula grew louder as Charlotte walked. She was sure she would come out on the other side of the woods soon.

After about fifteen minutes, she saw what looked like a building, patches of white paint visible through the green leaves.

Most of the house's windows had been broken, leaving gaping holes ringed with jagged glass teeth. Thick moss covered the fieldstones that made up most of the building.

Charlotte tried opening the porch door. Locked. She peeked through one of the windows, cupping her hands around her eyes. The glass was cloudy with dirt, but she could make out the kitchen table, its top covered in red enamel. She'd have to find another way in.

The once-grand summer cottage had been built on Annisquam's highest point. And when Charlotte turned around, she saw that the view from the porch was of the ocean.

She walked around to the rear of the house. Next to the back door, which was also locked, stood an old stone well, covered with a slab of sheet iron. A small shed stood about twenty feet back from the well.

Soft from termites and years of rain, the shed's door creaked as Charlotte pushed it open, its bottom scraping the ground. She shined the flashlight inside to reveal a few dusty workbenches sitting on the hard dirt floor.

Then she saw something she could use. An iron crowbar hung from a hook above a shelf crowded with clay flowerpots. She'd use it to pry open the back door.

The bar was heavier than it looked and felt cold in her hand. The corroded iron left a stain on her skin the color of dried blood.

Charlotte climbed the concrete stairs and pushed the tip of the crowbar into the crack between the door and jamb, just beneath the door handle. Trying to remember how she'd seen Charles pry open a door, Charlotte pulled back on the bar, concentrating the leverage on the tip. On her second try she heard a sharp snap and the door creaked open on rusty hinges.

A wave of hot musty air wafted out of the house, the smell of a stale summer cabin when it's first opened in the spring. She stepped inside and shut the door behind her, remembering to take the crowbar with her so as not to leave evidence of where she'd been.

She was in the rear of the kitchen, near the entrance to the dining room. In front of her was the pantry, still stocked with glass jars of pickled beans and applesauce. Stacks of china plates and bowls crowded the open shelves.

Ruth Smith's letter to her nephew said she'd hidden the blue bottle in the root cellar. Charlotte was going to have to figure out where that was.

Roaming the first floor, she entered a sitting room, its over-stuffed sofa and chairs the same color as the sea. Pictures of proud sailing ships and bright Victorian gardens decorated the walls.

She went from room to room in search of a door leading to the cellar. She entered the kitchen again, running her fingers along the lower halves of the walls, in case the door might have been covered by the room's flowered wallpaper. She checked behind the black cast iron stove and the curvy old refrigerator. But she found nothing.

Discouraged, she pulled up a chair and sat down at the kitchen table. The sun was nearly below the horizon, its pink and orange light shining into the room. It reminded Charlotte of the golden windows. The setting sun's reflection, for a short time every day, transformed the house into a magical place.

The setting sun also meant that Charlotte wasn't going to make it home.

Making up her mind to find a place to sleep, grateful that she'd be able to stay in the house rather than in the cannery, or worse, outside with the mosquitoes, Charlotte climbed the stairs to the second floor.

The stairs were steep and winding, bending at two landings before ending at a narrow hallway. Four doors lined either side of the hall. Another door was at the far end. Most of them had been left open, the ones on the western side of the house emitting an orange glow.

The pine floorboards creaked beneath Charlotte's feet as she checked each room. One of the doors led to a large bathroom, complete with a claw-foot tub big enough to lie down in. Another was a girl's bedroom. Pink floral curtains softened the edges of the windows which, unlike in many of the other rooms, weren't broken. A narrow child's bed, white with four tall posts, sat in the center of a white braided rug.

Another door led to a linen closet still stocked with stacks of folded sheets and towels. When Charlotte came to the door at the end of the hallway she turned the black iron knob and was surprised to find that it opened right up.

Situated at the front of the house, it was a large bedroom. Six of its wide windows faced east, toward the mouth of the cove and the ocean. And unlike the view from the front porch, the view from the room was free of trees. Huge waves crashed on the rocks where the ocean and cove met. With darkness coming on, she could see the rotating beam from the lighthouse on Light Island. She decided she would sleep there.

Without electricity, the house grew dark quickly. Charlotte kept Ezra's flashlight beside her but didn't turn it on. She wanted to preserve the batteries for emergencies. She found an old taper candle stuck into a pewter holder and a book of matches in the bedside table.

The light from the candle cast ghostly shadows that danced and swayed with the slightest movement of air. Charlotte felt terrible that her grandparents would be in a panic wondering where she was. The police would be looking for her.

When her stomach began to snarl and gurgle, she realized that she hadn't eaten since lunchtime.

She used the candle to light her way as she tiptoed down the stairs, heading back to the pantry to see if there was anything in it that she'd be able to eat.

Charlotte spotted a painted step stool in the corner and pulled it over to one of the shelves. She placed her candle on an empty shelf so that its glow lit up the small room. Glass jars of tomatoes and blackberry jam lined the shelves in neat rows. There were beets and pickled beef in brine, carrots and deviled eggs. Just as she was about to put the stool away, a jar of peaches, on the opposite side of the pantry, caught her eye. Those, at least, sounded good.

Reaching across the shelf with her right arm, Charlotte grabbed the jar and pulled it toward her. When she had it securely in her hand and was about to climb down she noticed something.

In the dim glow of the candlelight she saw the outline of a trap door in the pantry floor.

Putting the candle down, Charlotte grasped the door's metal ring and gave it a strong pull.

The smell of damp earth filled the small room.

Chapter 27

From where he sat beside the rocky cliffs outside the Annisquam Fish Cannery, Ezra kept a careful eye on the eel that had been assigned to watch him. He was waiting for a chance to run.

After Charlotte had fallen asleep, he'd gone outside to look for a way to get to the back of the cannery. One of Bathyal's eels had spotted him from where it was hiding among the rocks. The awful creature grabbed him from behind while another one covered his mouth so he couldn't warn Charlotte.

Ezra had no idea where Charlotte was, and no way of finding out if she was OK. If she had been able to get home he hoped she would send help. He hoped she didn't think he'd abandoned her.

The eel guarding Ezra leaned against a flat outcropping of rock, its eyes focused on something in the middle distance, out at sea.

Ezra wondered what the eel was staring at—and if it was distracting enough for him to try to make a run for it. If he was able to escape soon, before it was completely dark, he'd have a chance of getting home before Bathyal came back. He'd gone back to town, saying he'd return to get Ezra in a few hours.

When the eel turned away from the horizon, Ezra pretended to be asleep. The less active the eel thought he was, the better.

Keeping his eyes closed, Ezra imagined the exact route he would take. He was a good climber, and fast. He wouldn't have any trouble getting away if he got enough of a head start.

When the eel returned its gaze to the sea Ezra made his move.

He jumped up. At the edge of the cliff Ezra made a daring leap onto the rocks below—farther than he'd ever jumped—and landed on his feet. Without looking behind him, he scrambled across the rocks. He climbed up and over columns of granite, finding footholds as he went.

By the time he'd made it halfway back to town, it had grown almost completely dark. The western horizon was a pink line, the street lights and lit houses of Rocky Harbor visible in the distance. He knew there were eels following him, but if he could make it into town he'd be safe. He'd go into Barnacle Bob's restaurant, which was sure to be busy this time of night, and use the phone to call his grandmother.

Ezra was thinking of this when he hopped down from a particularly tall outcropping of rocks, near the spot where he and Charlotte had stopped to rest earlier that day. His sneaker got caught in a crevice between two large rocks and he twisted his ankle.

Pain shot up Ezra's leg, but he didn't dare make a sound. With both hands behind his knee, he was able to pull his foot free. He didn't think it was broken, but it hurt like hell.

Just when he'd recovered enough to keep going, Ezra felt a cold, wet hand clamp down on his shoulder. The eel that had been watching him stood over him. Beside it was another larger eel that he hadn't seen before. Ezra's hopes sank. He was so close, only a few hundred feet from Barnacle Bob's.

The larger eel said something Ezra couldn't understand, then grabbed him by the arm and began pulling him up. Just as they were getting ready to drag him off, Ezra's eye caught the water bottles Charlotte had taken out of her backpack that afternoon. Not believing his good luck, Ezra bent down, grabbed one of the bottles and popped the cap.

Holding the bottle in front of him, Ezra squeezed as hard as he could, hitting the larger eel directly in the eyes with a stream of fresh water.

A sizzling sound rose from the eel's flesh and the hideous creature let out a horrible scream. The second eel, seeing what had happened, began to back away.

Ezra grabbed another bottle. Keeping its nozzle aimed at the second eel, he backed slowly over the rocks in the direction of town. Clutching the plastic bottle, he finally limped onto the crushed stone parking lot outside of Barnacle Bob's. As he had predicted, the place was jammed with people.

As Ezra was about to go inside to use the phone, a Rocky Harbor police cruiser pulled into the lot. A uniformed officer, even taller than Ezra, got out of the car and headed toward Barnacle Bob's front door. When the police officer spotted Ezra, he stopped.

"Are you Ezra Bouchard?"

Ezra's face and arms were smudged with dirt, his shirt torn at the collar. In his left hand he still held the nearly empty water bottle.

"Yes."

"The whole town's been looking for you and Charlotte Hale. Where have you been? Did something happen? Where's Charlotte?"

Ezra exhaled, fatigue seeping into his bones. His ankle throbbed. "She was with me," he said, "but we got separated. We were out on the rocks by the cannery. I thought maybe she had come home on her own."

"Well if she has, I haven't heard about it. Why don't you get in the cruiser and I'll give you a ride home. Mrs. B's worried sick."

The whole way home all Ezra could think about was Charlotte. She could be anywhere, caught by the eels or stuck someplace in the cannery, pinned beneath one of the sections of steel ceiling that had fallen during the last tremor. He was going to have to find a way to go back out and find her.

Mrs. Bouchard came to the door wearing a pink house dress. When she saw her grandson a flood of relief washed over her worried face.

"Thank you, Daniel," she said to the officer.

"Ezra, where in the world have you been? It's after ten o'clock. Where's Charlotte? You know better than to stay out so late and not tell anyone where you are. Charlotte's grandfather has been calling all night. He's worried half to death."

Ezra inhaled and said, "We need to talk. I don't know where Charlotte is. I think something bad might have happened to her."

"What do you mean? Was there an accident?"

"I'm not even sure where to begin," said Ezra, finally sitting down. "You know the story you tell the kids, the one about Oceanus and Mortimer and the blue bottle? About the shipwreck in the Cove?"

Mrs. B set a ham sandwich down in front of him. "Yes, of course."

"Well, it's all true," said Ezra.

His grandmother sat down at the table beside him. "You're going to have to explain what you mean."

By the time Ezra finished telling her the story, from the cryptic messages written on Charlotte's dock to the eels that had been following them, it was after 11 o'clock.

Mrs. B sat back in her chair, crossing her arms in front of her. "It's possible that Charlotte is in danger. We're going to have to go back out to Annisquam to find her as soon as it's light. I know a path that leads to the old house."

Chapter 28

Charlotte peered down into the open trap door. A rickety wooden ladder led down to the cellar. Knowing she wasn't likely to find anything down there at night, even with the flashlight, she closed the door and decided to come back in the morning.

As she lay in the large bed, Charlotte listened to the bell buoy clanging at the entrance to the cove. The sound was so familiar it was almost as if she was in her own room. But she was a world away.

Charlotte woke with the first rays of sunlight breaking over the eastern horizon. She did her best to make the bed exactly the way she'd found it. In the bathroom, she was surprised to find that the cold tap still worked. She filled the sink and splashed cool water on her face, rinsed out her mouth and bent down to get a drink from the faucet.

Downstairs, the kitchen was bright and cheerful, the sun chasing away the gloominess of the night before. Charlotte pried the lid off the jar of preserved peaches and ate them at the kitchen table out of the container with a fork made from real silver she had found in a drawer.

When she finished eating, Charlotte turned her attention to the trap door. Pulling it open, she tucked Ezra's flashlight under her arm and began climbing down the ladder.

The cellar floor was made of dirt. And even though Charlotte wasn't very tall, the ceiling was so low she had trouble standing up straight.

Water pipes and cloth-covered electrical wiring, thick with cobwebs, ran along the ceiling—additions to the house after it had been built. Any food that had once been stored in the cellar had long ago rotted away or been scavenged by animals. Little remained in the cramped, dank room except for a collection of old crockery pots lined up on the sill.

Charlotte rubbed her palms on her forearms to ward off the dampness. Turning on the flashlight, she checked every ceiling beam, every crevice in the foundation, but came up with nothing.

Disappointed, Charlotte climbed back up the ladder to the pantry and closed the trap door behind her. The entire trip had been a waste of time. She was going to have to go home and explain why she'd been out all night. Her grandparents weren't going to be happy. They might even send her back to live with her father and Diane for the rest of the summer.

Remembering she'd left her earrings on the bedside table, Charlotte went upstairs to get them before heading home.

Just as it had been the first time she entered the room, the view of the ocean from the bedroom windows was spectacular. In the far distance she could see a cargo ship, a tiny gray block, on the horizon.

Beside her earrings, Charlotte found a pair of antique brass binoculars. Holding them up to her eyes, the cargo ship was transformed from a distant shape into a wide, steel vessel loaded with multicolored shipping containers.

Setting the binoculars down, Charlotte noticed something else she hadn't seen before. On the far left side of the room, set atop the sash of the last window, was something small and blue. The light from the morning sun caught the tiny bottle, about the size of a silver dollar, making it glow like a jewel.

Charlotte approached the bottle slowly, wondering how long it had been there—out in the open for anyone to see.

When she picked the bottle up, it felt heavy for its size. The glass was thick and wavy. It was the deepest azure blue she had ever seen.

But how could she tell if it was the real thing?

As she debated with herself about what to do, Charlotte heard the roar of waves crashing on a beach. But she was too far away from the shore to hear the surf, and besides, all the windows were closed.

The sound was coming from the blue bottle.

She put the bottle down on the table in front of her and took a step back. The mirror was still in her backpack, which was someplace in the cannery. She had no way to call Eucla. She was going to have to get to the water and hope for the best, and fast.

Slipping the bottle into her front pocket, Charlotte took one last look out the room's wide windows—and froze. Coming toward the house, through the dense woods, was Morton Bathyal and four of his eels. The creatures loped through the brush looking like the landed fish that they were, losing their balance with almost every stride. Bathyal urged them on, hollering in his thick English accent each time one of them stumbled.

She had to get out of the house.

Rushing downstairs, Charlotte tried to formulate a plan. If she went out the rear door where she'd come in, Bathyal was sure to see her as he came out of the woods. The front door was her only option.

Unlocking the front door from the inside, Charlotte stepped out onto the porch. The summer morning was sweet and warm, the clean smell of the sea on the breeze. She ran down the steps in the direction of the shore.

Wishing they were able to walk faster, Ezra followed his grandmother down the overgrown path that led to the part of the Annisquam Peninsula that lay behind the cannery. They had parked on the side of a dead-end dirt road that Ezra hadn't even known existed.

"We used to come down here all the time when we were kids," Mrs. Bouchard said, patting her brow with a folded bandana. She gripped a smooth birch walking stick in her right hand. She had worn her only pair of jeans and her best walking shoes. "Hardly anyone knows about this path anymore from the looks of it."

The narrow trail was choked with thorny blackberry brambles and wild sea roses. Poison ivy sprawled out along the ground in several places, wrapping its toxic vines around the trunks of birch trees and scrub pines. Ezra's grandmother held back the brush with her stick so they could pass without getting scratched or poisoned.

Soon the path began to angle downhill, forcing Ezra to check his footing on the loose, sandy soil. He hoped more than anything Charlotte had made it to the old house safely, and that they would find her when they got there.

When they finally arrived at the clearing where the house stood Mrs. Bouchard said, "I haven't been here since I was a girl. It looks almost the same."

She ran her hand over the heavy piece of steel that covered the well. "This used to be open," she said. "We'd hike through the woods and stop here to get a drink."

They looked around the yard, finding no evidence that Charlotte, or anyone else, had been there. Ezra climbed onto the porch and looked in the window. On the kitchen table he saw an empty canning jar with a fork beside it.

"Look!" Ezra called to his grandmother.

Mrs. Bouchard peeked through the glass and then tried the handle on the front door. It swung open almost before she could turn it.

"Someone was just here," she said, poking her head into the pantry. "The shelves have been disturbed. And look." She bent down and picked up from the floor something silver and shiny. It was an earring.

"That's Charlotte's!" said Ezra. "Looks like we just missed her. I bet she started for home when the sun came up."

"It does look like she was just here," said Mrs. Bouchard, "but it's hard to say where she went. Didn't you say that she thought the bottle was hidden here someplace?"

"Yes, but …"

"Where do you suppose she would go if she found it?"

"She would bring it down to the water," said Ezra, "to the ocean."

His grandmother nodded. "I think we need to check the ocean path."

Chapter 29

Charlotte ran through the woods toward the sound of the waves crashing on the rocks. Low branches flung themselves against her arms and chest like whips. A long, red scratch stretched across her cheek, tiny dots of blood rising to the surface. She didn't know if Bathyal or the eels had seen her, or if they were following her, but she didn't want to stop to find out.

The blue bottle felt heavy in her front pocket, like one of the lead fishing weights Charles used. She longed to take it out and look at it, to hear the sound of the waves coming from the tiny opening at its neck—as if somehow it contained the entire ocean inside of it. But she kept running.

By the time she'd gone just a few hundred yards, the trees began to thin out. The sound of the surf grew louder. Charlotte could smell the sea.

Pushing apart the last few saplings, Charlotte stepped out onto the crest of a bluff overlooking the ocean. She was at the very tip of the peninsula. She had to find a way to climb down.

Scanning the rocks from left to right, she noticed a part of the cliff that seemed less treacherous than the rest, still dangerous, but possible to navigate if she was careful.

Charlotte stretched her right leg down to find a foothold. She wasn't going to be able to go very fast, but she would get to the water. She hoped there would be a safe place for her to stand once she got there.

After she'd climbed about twenty feet down the cliff, her fingers red and aching, Charlotte heard voices.

"I think she went this way!" The garbled, gurgling speech of one of Bathyal's eels echoed through the trees. They had followed her by using the path of bent branches and crushed undergrowth she'd left behind to track her down.

The water was only another 25 feet away.

Then they spotted her.

"Here! Hurry! She's trying to get to the water!"

Not knowing what else to do, Charlotte kept climbing downward, reminding herself to go slowly. Falling to her death onto the rocks below wouldn't do anyone any good.

One of the eels began climbing down after her. He wasn't going much faster than she was, but she knew if she didn't hurry he'd catch up to her before she made it to the shoreline.

Ezra and his grandmother left the old house and continued down the ocean path, which didn't look much like a trail, more like a narrow gap in the trees, Ezra thought. Barely discernible at its opening, the path had been so neglected that at its widest point it wasn't much more than a foot across. They had to walk single file, brushing against branches as they went, one foot in front of the other.

"Grandma?"

"Yes, Ezra." She swung her walking stick to the side to push a low-hanging conifer branch out of the way.

"I forgot to tell you. You might need this." He took one of the bottles of water he had in his backpack and handed it to her.

"Thank you," she said. "A drink would be nice."

"Actually, that's not what it's for."

Mrs. Bouchard stopped walking and turned to look at him. "What is it for then?"

"To protect yourself. From the eels."

Raising her eyebrows, she took the water and put it in her pack. She let out a deep sigh. "As long as I've lived there are still so many things I've yet to learn, Ezra. Keep that in mind for yourself."

Just when Ezra was getting used to walking sideways, the path came to an abrupt end. He and his grandmother stood atop a high vista overlooking the sea.

"I never knew this was here," he said.

"It's the uppermost point of Rocky Harbor. The head of the Annisquam," said Mrs. Bouchard. "The Native Americans believed this spot was sacred."

It wasn't hard for Ezra to see why. The sky met the sea over a dramatic grouping of cliffs, like something you'd expect to see in a movie. Nothing stood between them and the Portuguese coast but the wide, green Atlantic.

They had been walking along the top of the cliff for a few minutes when they heard voices.

"You. Get down there. Quickly. There is to be no chance she'll get away."

Ezra's skin went cold. The voice was Morton Bathyal's. They were after Charlotte.

"We have to help her," said Ezra, lowering his voice.

"Don't do anything yet," said Mrs. Bouchard. She grabbed the tail of Ezra's polo shirt to squelch any impulse he might have to run. "We need to see what's going on before you go out there. They'll be on you in a second."

Ezra peered out from behind a slim maple tree. Morton Bathyal was standing at the top of the cliff wearing his customary dark suit.

Chapter 30

Two eels were now climbing down the cliff after Charlotte, the closest one just six feet away from the top of her head. Knowing she needed to hurry, she lowered her right foot and found a toehold in the cliff. But when she put her weight on it the rock gave way.

An avalanche of gravel and debris tumbled into the sea beneath her feet. Rocks splashed into the water, leaving empty space in the spot where her feet would have come to rest. She hung from the cliff by her fingertips. Unsure of how long she'd be able to hold on, she knew that even if she were strong enough to pull herself back up, the eels were gaining on her.

Seeing her distress, the closest eel picked up its pace, hoping to catch her before she recovered.

With the eel just feet away, Charlotte let go of the cliff and let herself fall. She pushed away from the cliff with her feet at the last second, hoping to propel herself far enough out so that she'd land in the water rather than on the rocks.

As she fell, a feeling of calm came over her. She wasn't afraid. And though she knew it must only have been a few seconds, the fall felt long and slow.

Hitting the water knocked the breath out of her lungs.

Plunging into the cold, salty sea, Charlotte opened her eyes and began swimming toward the surface.

When her head broke through the waves she heard someone calling her name, "Charlotte!"

Treading water, she looked from one side of the cliff top to the other. It was Ezra! And Mrs. Bouchard! She tried calling to them, but ended up swallowing a mouthful of water.

"Call Eucla! Hurry!" Ezra yelled down to her. It was only then Charlotte noticed that both eels were just a few feet away from the bottom of the cliff. Morton Bathyal was close behind them. If they jumped into the water after her they would have her for sure.

Charlotte took the bottle from her pocket and held it under the water. "Eucla, I've got it," she said. "Please hurry."

Numb from the cold and unable to tread water much longer, she swam over to a group of rocks and hauled herself out. She kept her eyes on the waves, waiting for a sign of the mermaid.

Charlotte felt a hand on the back of her neck.

Morton Bathyal's skin was cold and slippery, like the scaly covering of a fish.

"Ah, Charlotte," he said, pulling her up. "Look at the trouble you've caused yourself. That was a nasty fall. You might have been killed."

Charlotte struggled to break free, but Bathyal was too strong.

"I think you'll find once you give me what I want you'll have sufficient help getting off this rock and back home," Bathyal said. "And please, don't act as if you don't have what I'm looking for. It will save us both a lot of time."

Charlotte didn't notice that Ezra had also climbed down the cliff and was coming up behind them. With a bottle of water in each hand, he waited until he was a few feet away from Bathyal's back before he aimed and squeezed. The water shot out, soaking Bathyal's suit jacket.

He let out a howl as smoke rose up from the wound the water burned into his flesh. Bathyal dropped to his knees, unable to speak. His face was purple with pain.

One of the eels lurched forward to take Bathyal's place.

Ezra moved to block the eel's path, but when he aimed his water bottle at it he saw that it was empty.

A second eel came out from behind the first, shoving Ezra aside. Ezra fell, smacking his head against the rocks with an awful thud.

Afraid for her life and Ezra's, Charlotte took the blue bottle out of her pocket and prepared to hand it over. Eucla hadn't come. No one had.

The thick blue glass was smooth and cool in her hand. She was about to hand the bottle to Bathyal when something big leapt up from beneath the surface of the water.

It was as large as a dolphin and moving so fast that Charlotte didn't realize that Eucla had come to her rescue until the mermaid was on top of one of the eels. Her silver tail thrashed in the sun as she sank her frightening claws into the monster's flesh. As quick as a fish, she bent forward and took a ferocious bite out of the eel, leaving a yawning wound. The creature sank to the rocks.

With one eel down, Eucla turned her sights on the second. Even out of the water, her strength was fearsome as she launched herself at it, claws and teeth extended. Seeing it was no match for the mermaid, the eel made a running leap into the water.

Eucla dove into the ocean after it, disappearing beneath the waves. The sea churned and boiled until the water turned red with blood. Charlotte waited, but Eucla didn't resurface. A terrible, sinking feeling settled in her stomach.

Swift, gray storm clouds raced in from all directions, blocking out the sun. The air temperature dropped and the sky crackled with lightning. A thunderous boom shook the ground, and the wind blew with such force that the surface of the ocean turned flat, clumps of seaweed flying like dry leaves along the shore.

Morton Bathyal stood up, the wound on his back almost completely healed. His voice was softer, less demanding, "Charlotte, have some sense, child. You have no idea what you're doing with that bottle. Your mermaid friend is gone. And just look at the sky. Do you know how many fishermen will be caught in the storm you've created? I'm sure most of them have families just like yours."

Knowing she was beaten, Charlotte offered the bottle to Bathyal. Even in the sunless sky, the small glass container gleamed like a sapphire.

Seeing the bottle in the center of Charlotte's palm, Mortimer's eyes grew wide. In another moment he would have control over

124

the world's oceans and all the creatures in them. And there was nothing anyone would be able to do to stop him.

Then, as suddenly as they appeared, the storm clouds began to break up. The wind stopped blowing and the air became still.

On the cliff top, Charlotte spotted a fisherman. His yellow oilskin pants were held in place by black suspenders. He was clean-shaven, his hair cut short. As he gazed toward the horizon, he looked neither young nor old, but had the look of the sea about him, like a man who has spent his life on the water.

The fisherman walked to the edge of the cliff and turned so that his back was facing the sea. He crouched down, as if he were about to begin climbing down the cliff. But instead of extending a leg to find a foothold in the rock, he launched himself backward, pushing away from the cliff top with his legs. He was airborne.

Charlotte gasped as the yellow-clad figure fell away from the cliff side. She winced, not wanting to see him plunge to his death on the rocks below.

But the fisherman didn't fall. Like a paper airplane, he glided downward circling over their heads until he set his rubber boots gently on the ground beside Charlotte and Ezra, where Morton Bathyal stood fixated on the small, blue object in Charlotte's hand.

The fisherman said, "Thank you for keeping my bottle safe, Charlotte. I know it was a difficult task."

Snatching the bottle out of Bathyal's reach, Charlotte held the blue bottle out to the fisherman. "You're welcome."

The fisherman took the bottle and slipped it into his pocket. "I give you my word that I, and all the creatures of the sea, will forever be at your service."

Charlotte looked out at the spot where she had last seen Eucla. "I don't want anything. Just please help Eucla."

The fisherman's blue eyes twinkled. "Don't worry about the sea people," he said. "Your friend Eucla will soon be made well again."

With that, the fisherman reached out and grasped Morton Bathyal, his brother, by the arm.

"I banished you to the bottom of the ocean for defying me, and yet it seems you have not learned your lesson. You and your eels shall be cursed to walk the land forever, never again returning to the sea."

Facing the ocean, the fisherman, who was Oceanus, the god of the sea, raised his arms above his head and called out a phrase so ancient that only the rocks and the waves knew its meaning.

The red eels came up from the water in droves, their snakelike bodies thrashing on the rocks.

"Brother, I know I have wronged you, but spare them. They are simple creatures," said Mortimer.

"Very well," said Oceanus. "You and Anguilla shall roam the earth alone."

An enormous wave, nearly as tall as the cliffs themselves, washed the eels back into the sea.

Defeated, Morton Bathyal, a large hole in the back of his suit jacket, began walking toward the cliff. Anguilla, who had avoided the action below, waited for him at the top.

They disappeared into the Annisquam woods.

Oceanus reached into his pocket and pulled out a pink scallop shell. He handed it to Charlotte. "Should you ever need my help again throw this into the sea."

He bent down to retie the laces on one of his boots and began to walk out into the water until it completely covered him. Then he was gone.

Chapter 31

"What time is everyone supposed to get here?" asked Charlotte. She sat at the kitchen table, running her finger around the rim of a glass of milk while Gram put the finishing touches on her father and Diane's wedding cake.

"The ceremony is at one o'clock," said Gram, her attention focused on the pink and blue icing flowers circling the cake's top tier. "We've got a few hours. Why don't you go outside and see if your brother and Grandpa need help, then you can get dressed."

Out in the yard, Grandpa and Charles had set up several rows of white folding chairs before a latticework arch that would serve as the backdrop for the wedding ceremony. Although Charlotte wasn't very happy about the wedding itself, she had to admit that the setting was beautiful, especially with the cove in the background.

There was no sign of Charles or her grandfather, so Charlotte climbed out onto the dock and sat down. The letters Eucla had carved into the wood were still there. Charlotte felt like a whole different person than on the day she had first seen them, even though it had been only two months ago.

"Hey, kiddo."

Charlotte turned to find her father stepping out onto the dock behind her. He had on his tuxedo pants and shirt, but was missing his jacket and tie. Instead of dress shoes, he wore a pair of rubber flip-flops.

"Those shoes don't match," said Charlotte, pointing to his feet. "I thought you were upstairs getting ready."

"I was," said her father, "but I thought maybe we could talk a minute."

Charlotte nodded.

"Gram told me about what happened with your mom the day you took the bus out to her house." He bent down and brushed a section of the dock clean with his hand before sitting down. "I'm sorry about that."

Charlotte said, "Dad I …"

"Wait, let me finish. Your grandparents and I have been talking and we think it would be a good idea for you and Charles to live here next year and go to Cape Ann Regional High School. It will give you a chance to have a new start—like you wanted with your mom. Charles can help Grandpa out on his new boat after school and on weekends."

"But what about you? What will you and Diane do?" said Charlotte.

"Well, we're thinking about going out West for a while, to Arizona maybe. Chloe's going to go live with her dad."

"So you're leaving us?" Charlotte stood up, not wanting to hear any more.

"It won't be forever, Charlotte. Just until we get settled as a married couple. A lot of people do it. We're looking for a new start, just like you."

Charlotte stood at the end of the dock closest to the house, arms crossed, looking down at her father. Behind him, she saw the surface of the cove erupt into hundreds of tiny bubbles. A pale arm, and then an entire head, emerged from the water.

Eucla looked at Charlotte and held her index finger up to her lips.

"Fine," said Charlotte to her father, trying to ignore Eucla, who swam toward the dock without making so much as a tiny splash. "I like living here. I have my own room and Gram and Grandpa take good care of me. In fact, I think I should live here permanently."

Her father stood up and opened his mouth to speak, but before he could say anything Eucla reached out and grabbed his ankle. With her enormous strength, she pulled him into the water in one swift motion.

When he came back to the surface, Charlotte's father was choking and sputtering. His carefully styled hair looked like the fur on a wet dog.

"God damn it!" he yelled, hauling himself out of the water. "My shirt and pants are ruined! Now what am I supposed to wear?"

Brushing past Charlotte, he hurried across the yard. "Ma! Help! I need to dry my pants!"

Gram met him at the door and let him in.

"Thanks, Eucla," Charlotte said, smiling. "Thank you. Thank you."

Chapter 32

"Hey, are you almost ready? We should try to get there a little early." Charles stood outside Charlotte's bedroom door, a brand new backpack slung over his shoulder.

"Be down in two minutes," said Charlotte, smoothing her shirt in the mirror. Her stomach was so full of butterflies that she'd had to force herself to eat the bowl of Cheerios Gram had put in front of her. It had been a long time since she'd gone to a new school, and even longer since she'd been someplace where she knew absolutely no one. The only kid she'd met all summer in Rocky Harbor was Ezra and he'd gone home to New Hampshire a week ago.

Edward Kitchen was at the bus stop when Charlotte and Charles arrived. He sat on the curb by himself reading a paperback sci-fi novel.

"Hi, Edward!" said Charlotte.

"Oh, hi, Charlotte!" said Edward, surprised to see her. "I didn't know you were going to school here this year. How did your summer project turn out?"

"Summer project?...oh, that summer project. It turned out great, thanks. It was a lot more work than I thought it was going to be, though, that's for sure."

The school bus rumbled around the corner. The wheeze of its transmission overpowered the quiet sounds of the early morning. The brakes let out a squeak as it pulled up to the sidewalk.

"Great service," said Edward, standing up. "Right on time." He pulled his bus pass out of the front pocket of his backpack.

Charlotte, Edward and Charles went to the back of the line. The two kids in front of them, a set of twins named Amy and Ivy, had begun boarding the bus when she heard someone calling her name.

"Charlotte! Tell the bus driver to wait up!"

Running down the street, his long legs making quick work of the distance, was Ezra.

Out of breath, Ezra got to the bus stop just as the last of the kids were getting on.

"What are you doing here? Why aren't you in New Hampshire?" said Charlotte as Ezra slid into the seat beside her.

"My mom decided to sell the store and move down here. My grandmother's got such a big house. And the store has been a lot of work for her since my dad died. She's going to open a new shop downtown. I hear there's an empty space where the antique store used to be." Ezra set his backpack down on the floor. "I guess it sort of helped that I kept telling her about how great it was in Rocky Harbor – how I got a job, and found a really awesome friend."

"Who's that?" said Charlotte, wondering if Ezra had met someone she didn't know about.

Ezra looked at her.

"Ohhh," said Charlotte, her cheeks flushing red.

Ezra put his arm around Charlotte's shoulders as the bus rolled toward the high school. Outside the window, the water in the cove reflected the morning sun like a thousand tiny mirrors.

About the Author

Emilie-Noelle Provost is a magazine editor, columnist and features writer who lives in northeastern Massachusetts with her husband, daughter and four crazy rescue cats. She is a lifelong lover of books who believes that stories are essential for a healthy, happy life. You can find out more about her work at emilienoelleprovost.com.

About the Illustrator

Lucy Turner is an artist living in Scotland, UK. She lives with her husband and is mother to two children. Lucy creates her work using watercolors, colored pencils, gouache and ink. She would describe her work as quirky yet ethereal and with a childlike quality. Her favorite things to draw are faces, eyes and the moon and her work often features surreal elements and inspiration from nature. Lucy's work is often moody, brooding and dark but other times can be bright and colorful. Her inspirations change often and can be reflected in her style. When Lucy is not making art, she loves to write, listen to music and spend time in her kitchen cooking and baking. Her favorite color is green and she finds spending time in nature and among plants the best way to recharge.

CPSIA information can be obtained
at www.ICGtesting.com
Printed in the USA
BVHW07s1508280918
528638BV00003B/12/P